ANNE Z☀ELLE

Tender of the GARDEN

EXCELSINE PRESS

Other Books by Anne Zoelle:

The Awakening of Ren Crown

The Protection of Ren Crown

The Rise of Ren Crown

The Unleashing of Ren Crown

The Destiny of Ren Crown

House of Scepters

Cage of Shadows

Crown of Starlight

Contents

Chapter One: The Dome

The dome stretched over her, crackling and swirling with ghostly white light. It was her sanctuary and prison; her commitment and sacrifice.

Lush vines twined lovingly around her as shabby beastlets and gloriously built creatures prowled the outermost ley circle surrounding the dome's perimeter. The dark energy and magical promise of divine ability called them forth.

A group of macaw-emus with brilliantly bejeweled heads and necks atop large, flightless bodies brushed the edges of the magic and transformed into their hybrid antithesis—emu-macaws with small heads, large eyes, and swift, long-tailed forms. They flew gracefully up into the erythrina trees and their glorious red tail feathers glittered in the rays of filtered sunlight.

The ears of a panther-wolf twitched suddenly, its easy lope frozen as it approached the outermost circle, one paw hovering over one of the eight ley lines embedded in the earth that symmetrically converged on the Nexus at the center of the dome. The predator jerked back, stumbled, and fled, setting every animal around it in motion. The grove emptied in sudden terror as the Northeastern Ley vibrated in warning.

The vines clinging to her slid along her skin in anticipation. Soon, soon, they said in the language of the garden.

Lirah ran her hand along their spiked bodies and waited for the monster that all feared.

The purple oaks shook above him, shedding their crisp bronze leaves and leaving a soft brass sheen to the canopy as he emerged from the dense brush. Bronze fell in feathered tears from the sky, mixing with the purple, green, and rose of the felm trees and the turquoise of the fanlee bushes.

The massive creature prowled forth over the fallen foliage. Lethal claws and shifting indigo scales glinted under the rays of sunlight piercing through the trees, then darkened again in shadow.

Impenetrable wings were tucked beneath equally impenetrable scales. In this form, his ability to take down anything he wished within fighting range invalidated the use of aerial needs.

"Magnificent," she whispered.

There was hunger in his eyes as he prowled sinuously toward her, but even though he had been lured to the dome consistently since the Trigger, not the faintest hint of recognition appeared. Prized and feared in this form—even his own kin ran from him when he was unleashed, fleeing ahead of the devastation he always left behind.

In this magically-induced and uncontrollable form, fiercer than any predator hybrid ever known, Set Tyrne, the Dark Prince of the Cruel Lands, never left survivors.

And at the completion of the current moon cycle, he would be the instrument of her death.

His predatory gaze didn't leave hers, and his spade tale swung in a mesmerizing rhythm that she had seen countless opponents fall before. Piranha-sharp teeth, and talon edged ears created a reasonable backdrop to the copious amounts of blood striping his body.

"Do you think you will break through this time, Berserker?"

He snarled.

"You will not."

He launched himself at the dome. Lightning crackled across the curvature, electrocuting him every time he touched it, but the pain never made him pause.

Lirah stepped closer and placed her left hand against the magic, trying to feel the echo of the shocks—to feel something, anything, from the outside world—then slid her gaze along the perimeter of the grove, an instinctive check to make certain no one was watching. But the action was unwarranted. No one risked being near Set Tyrne in this form.

She pressed harder, trying to feel the reverberations of magic or the touch of his skin. There were no leykeepers or kingservants to watch or berate her for her misconduct. In these moments...in these moments, she was free.

With her other hand, she stroked the plants twining around her—let them wrap her palm and the back of her hand. The rough texture on the backside of a leaf rolled and turned to caress her with its satin-smooth front. The tip of the leaf drew along her wrist, its red venom tip skating along her flesh, but not breaking the skin.

Creatures and magical beings were, to a one, terrified of the beast raging against the barrier of the dome. But she, who was surrounded by deadly things, thought him magnificent.

He clawed wildly at the magic of her enclosure. But made of creation magic at its densest levels, there was no creature in the five kingdoms—not even one such as Set Tyrne—that could penetrate it.

Until the Renewal Moon. The sacrifice. Her sacred duty.

Finally, spent, Set collapsed onto the mossy carpet between leys, his impenetrable scales glinting as he breathed heavily.

She crouched in front of the interior ley circle and placed a hand on cold metal. It warmed immediately beneath her palm and a tiny amount of the magic she was allotted each day shot out along the ley line, spreading and warming the grass outside the dome.

Her magic healed his wounds as he returned slowly to his human form.

In the moonlight, scales and silver scars glinted just beneath the surface of his skin as he covered his face with his hands.

In a moon cycle of the past, he would never have shown such vulnerability. He would not have cared. Dark Prince of the Cruel Lands—no one had earned a title more.

She touched him again with the only thing she could—the magic that ran between the inside and outside of her prison and sanctuary.

"I can't stop it," he said—her love, her death, her enemy mere moons ago—in the rough voice she cherished most, even after becoming reacquainted with the beautiful sounds of the outside world.

When the growing moon reached its peak fullness, the magic of the dome would cease for the few moments her death would take, and the man in front of her would not recognize her until long after she lay dead upon the garden's floor.

"I can't stop it," he repeated.

Her hand stroked the ley, soothing him in the only way that she could. "I know."

Chapter Two: The Ways

Three full moons ago...

The eight leykeepers, dressed in ornamental leathers, approached the gold-lined circle surrounding the enchanted dome. They were in human form, but their eyes contained the shadows of their beasts.

Each took his designated spot around the exterior ley circle.

The first keeper pressed a pendant against his ley point at the circle's border. Lirah held herself still and kept her expression calm, even as her breath caught in anticipation of sound. Their visits were the only times that communication existed between the dome and the outside world. She had heard no other voice but theirs in seventy-two moon cycles.

"Tender," he said in the musical language of the southern butterfly people.

"Leykeeper." She nodded first to him, then turned a slow circle to nod to the others who had pressed their pendants against their own directional ley points. "Leykeepers."

"Tender," the keeper of the southwest answered in the harsh tones of the bison-wolves, rulers of the plains. "The Long Moon is nearly upon us, then the Elden, Hunger, and Renewal moons will rise to bring about your final crowned days. Are you ready for what the Hunger and Renewal will bring?"

The prick of a thorn, blood spun from gold; under the moon's eyes, a new tender will arise and the old will be forsworn.

"I will be ready." Ready for the beauty of sacrifice. For strengthening the lands and people of the five kingdoms. To be flayed upon the Nexus at the hands of its most celebrated prince.

To be transformed.

The two leykeepers eyed her critically—no doubt looking to see if she would create trouble in the sunset of her term—and she forced herself not to look at the others.

The butterfly hybrid gave a satisfied nod. "You have been a good tender. A credit to your people."

Quiet exultation flowed through her, nearly filling the hollow void that was always present. "Thank you."

"We have picked a fitting end for a glorious reign. Your sacrifice will be spoken of in reverence and awe for all eternity."

She watched his fingers make the hand gesture used freely throughout the Cruel Lands—a warding against, and blessing for, the monster they idolized.

"Set Tyrne?" She smiled calmly, for they were still watching her. "I am honored."

There was relief in the set of the butterfly's expression, but the bison watched her with narrowed, cautious eyes.

"It is a great honor," the latter said gruffly. "You will be exalted."

She smiled at him and his narrowed look loosened.

The other leykeeper looked between them briefly, then exchanged some unseen communication with one of the leykeepers on the other side of the dome, before focusing on her again. "Your access to the garden's magic will end at the apex of the full Renewal Moon, but the allotment of magic available to you will steadily increase until then. An honor, for your excellent service." Butterfly wings shot from his back as he bowed his head.

"Thank you, Leykeeper." She pushed aside any emotion detrimental to serenity and focused on what she could control. Pride in her work and excitement in the opportunity to use additional magic made her stand tall. It made the hollowness beneath those feelings harder to sense, and helped subdue the need to question her life and fate.

Someday, she would be the perfect tender who questioned nothing. She bowed. "May the gold in darkness transform you always."

"And may it soon transform you, Tender."

Her breath caught at the extra note of solemnity he infused, and the hollow filled, just a bit. The standard parting had never before applied to her—for she was a stagnant creation, unable to shift in the midst of creatures that wildly bloomed with every breath.

But for one moment in time—at her sacrifice—she would transform. The bittersweet promise from the ley priests who had taken her from her tribe so many moons before would be fulfilled.

The childish taunts of her youth—"Unchangelings never change!"—would ring in her mind no more.

Before the memories could take any hold, she quashed them under firm control and forced calm—through stiffening limbs kept immobile at her sides. "Yes."

Whatever expression she wore satisfied the leykeepers further. They bowed again—all eight of them—and lifted their amulets from their glistening directional ley points, then strode off separately into the impenetrable mist blanketing the edges of the grove.

The vines twined around her as she retreated to the center of the garden. The white mist settled completely around the dome, sealing her off from curious eyes.

Soon, sister, soon, the vines whispered against the moss and breeze.

She rubbed her right forefinger against her thumb. One prick, one drop of gold so long ago, had canonized her to this existence.

A life sentence. No tender had successfully fled the kingdoms after the Choosing, and none had escaped the dome in more than nine hundred moons of the garden's existence.

With us, with us, with us.

She caressed the venomous vines seeking her attention as they wound up and around her.

"I am with you, of course," she murmured softly, stroking them and letting their deadly tips drag along her skin.

Sad, why so sad?

"A stray bit of mind fear, worry not," she soothed.

Sensing her pensive mood, they twined more tightly around her, seeking comfort and companionship.

There were worse fates for a girl than seventy-five moons of green fellowship and exalted sacrifice, with the knowledge that her people were taken care of, glorified, and capable of the continuing magic they had relied upon since the Nexus had formed. There were worse fates than the promise of metamorphosis for a girl forever incapable of it.

There were far worse fates for an unchangeling.

She gripped her fingers into fists, and looked down at her arms, where the verdant hue of the vines' venom continuously bled beneath her skin.

She could feel the magic of the garden thrumming through her. The extra allotment must have been a reward already in the works, for she had felt the steady increase over the past few lunar cycles.

What she chose to do with her extra magic was an active question to decide. There was no time to waste on thoughts of the past.

The vines twined excitedly around her limbs as she stepped barefoot across the moss and sank next to the mirrored pool. Magic hovered in the leys and vines, vibrating in the wind, whispering suggestions for what she could do with it.

Blood sacrifice.

Revenge.

Elimination of threats.

Family.

The family of the tender was hand-served by the five kingdoms in gratitude for the tender's service and sacrifice. Lirah pulled her fingers through the pool, and resisted the urge to call up images of the eagliger tribe she had been born into. She already intimately knew the abundant, joyful images she would see in the village filled with proud half-eagle, half-tiger forms.

After being a drain on family resources for the first twelve years of her life, Lirah's sacrifice had made their lives comfortable and exalted.

One of the vines curled closer, seeking comfort.

She stroked it. "I am content," she murmured.

Her family...they had tried to love her—had tried to understand and meet the needs of the being they needed to hand-dispatch to and from their sky cave dwellings. Understanding had never been fully realized, but they celebrated her now—heralded her fiercely along with the rest of the tribe.

And if an edge of relief at her absence still existed, they could be forgiven for that. She had learned to be content.

The vine curled even closer.

She closed her eyes and forced herself to recall her father's voice when the leykeepers had taken her away. "We are proud of you, Lirah of the Eagligers," he had called out.

Lirah of the Eagligers—the first and last time she'd been referred to as such.

For now she was Tender of the Garden, revered and forsaken by all. The voiceless ghost of the garden that made the painless transformations of all the beings in the five kingdoms possible. A glorious task for a frail, unchangeling girl in a warriors' world.

She released some of her newly acquired magic, sending it blindly along the Western Ley to her family's village. A little extra for the young, a little something for the elders, a boosted measure for her parents and siblings.

First task completed, she forced the past to where it belonged and slid her fingers along the surface of the pool. The waters curled with long practice into an image of the sapfox village nestled in the brush and shade of the northwestern forest.

Propelling the moving images with a lazy figure eight pattern, she finally found the village's unchangeling child skipping moss stones along the flora of a less popular grove.

Despite the clever spots where the child sometimes hid, the foxlings with their enhanced senses usually found her, and Lirah watched them do so now, moving in from the edges of the rippling image.

"Change, change, change. Unchangelings never change."

Lirah could see their snapping canine teeth forming the words, even though the pool gifted her no sound.

Those taunts had been quelled by the village elders upon Lirah's choosing. But before that, she had needed to find ways to endure. This child, too, had learned. It was the way of the shift—the folktale message of Lacsha's Lament and Filius' Form. The strong and the powerful had the control, while those who were not lived by their wits or perished with inflexible spirit.

Magic wrapped around her, and her fingers moved in response to memories old and observations new. What people frequently overlooked in those tales was that nature was a fickle and bountiful force, and that sometimes it was watching.

Lirah touched the interior point of the ley beam that ran closest to the child, hundreds of leagues away from the garden. The child startled as a vine shot from the earth and wrapped around her palm.

Deadlier than the most venomous of snakes, every tribe in the five kingdoms knew a Caliverias vine was never to be trusted. The other children screamed and ran—transforming into their fox forms to flee faster.

Lirah smiled and softly nudged the water.

Unfurling around the girl's hand, the envenomed tip of the stalk burst into bloom and a gold-edged crystal tear fell into the girl's palm.

An awed and delighted smile echoed upon the girl's unchanging human face and her eyes went bright with moisture as her other hand joined the first to secure the offering. The vine sinuously retreated into the ground, leaving the small teardrop gem in her cupped hands.

Lirah pet the vine at her waist as the image of the girl rippled away.

So few knew the full extent of what the vines and garden could do. People feared the garden, but even the feldragons would live in terror if they knew that it wasn't only their berserker prince who could bring about destruction.

Prince of the Cruel Lands, Scourge of the North, Executioner—she wondered what blood soaked field he was bathed in today.

She outlined a claw in the water with her finger and flicked it. A fiercer, swirling magic pulled into place instead of the tranquil shimmer she had called for the girl.

No, the feldragons had little idea of what they'd agreed to by letting their fiercest warrior become the executioner for the leykeepers' designs.

She dove inside the pool, letting the image wrap around her in her descent. As she sank deeper, the last dot of color fit into place and the entire image opened into a landscape. She stepped onto the bloodstained grass of a battlefield.

She closed her eyes, soaking in the feeling of being free—even though it was a false reality. The entry point was visual only—the magic creating an illusion. But the ability to waterwalk had saved her from going mad long ago.

It was something that had gotten easier, too, the greater her tending of the garden and kingdoms had become.

She looked at the evidence of her work, ignoring the raging battle as she walked.

The Cruel Lands, the three segments of the leys the feldragons ruled—so named for past harsh wars fought over the lands, and the fierce inhabitants few crossed—were bursting with transformation magic under her fierce care. But although the garden's magic was vast, it still only extended to the ends of the leys and the five kingdoms within the circuit—five kingdoms that had, historically, been uneasy allies and frequent combatants. But rumors had turned uneasy allies into staunch comrades decades ago as waves of outside creatures and beings sought to control the vast magic of the garden and Nexus.

Evil things were heading their way in increasing numbers, and Set Tyrne was beckoned to the battlefield more than ever. And the feldragons, through him, were slowly gaining their own foothold into ruling all.

Barefoot and with a vine trailing behind her, Lirah finally looked at the combatants as she advanced as an invisible specter on the active, blood-drenched field.

The end of the Northeastern Ley was beneath her feet—feldragon territory—as species of all sorts swept and weaved violently together in a dancing loom of death around it, pushing at the boundaries of the territory.

Beings from the tropics had been active adversaries in three previous full moons. Enemies from the plains the three moons before. This cycle's opposing force looked to be mercenaries from the desert lands far to the east, as there was something heavy and water-laden in their changing forms.

All were combatants who had either not believed the rumors of certain death at the hands of the prince who guarded the Cruel Lands, or who were so desperate for fertile land or greater magic to aid their sluggish transformations, that they had chosen to risk taking such territory by force.

The battle was fierce. A poisoned blade passed through her invisible form. Lirah examined the blade as it sunk into an opponent. The impaled feldragon writhed desperately upon the ground, going in and out of his transformation, and nothing he forced into his lips to counteract the poison seemed to be doing him any good.

A new weapon, perhaps. A viral strain of poison might even make a difference in a kingdom without a true berserker. But this was not the reality of the enemy they chose to attack.

The greatest weapon in the five kingdoms was activated with a roar.

From the tree castles of the Great Forest, the feldragons guarded and ruled the Cruel Lands in their dragon and saber-toothed forms. And Set Tyrne, who had the rare, prized ability to shift into an additional form—a berserker form that was larger, fiercer, and completely without regard for life—was their finest instrument of death.

The spade tails of the feldragons waved sinuously behind them as they leaped to safety, sharp smiles on their ferocious faces. Their allies fled as well, though not as skillfully or practiced.

Oblivious to pain, heedless of injury, the berserking Dark Prince chose the shortest path to each opponent, ripping himself on their blades and claws before any opponent could deal a deliberate strike. Long ribbons of blood streaked from him as he tore through the battlefield.

Lirah cocked her head, observing the absolute terror on the faces of his enemies. The opposing forces had obviously not believed the gruesome rumors, and though they tried to run, within minutes of Set's unleashing, the battlefield was a wasteland of broken adversaries and death.

When not a single living being remained in a three-mile radius, the magnificent beast roared at his victory, then fell, twitching uncontrollably, as if he too had been poisoned.

Magic overload was unkind. And the more Lirah tended the kingdoms, the greater Set's magic grew.

She walked over to him and stood above his beastly form, watching with dispassionate eyes as the uncontrollable magic that overwhelmed him in his berserker form rippled over him in violent waves.

A few opportunistic enemies from extremely long range shot magic-dipped arrows toward him, looking to gain advantage in this moment of vulnerability. At the last second, a small burst of magic rippled from Set, splitting the arrows, and small, poisoned scales shot from him and sliced quickly through the air, taking the archers down. Though the berserker's self-preservation response reacted to the danger, he didn't rouse.

All further threats toward him stopped.

Slowly, healers from all species roped fallen troops from great distances and dragged them to the leys—working to heal or resurrect their salvageable troops far from the beast that could stir at any moment.

But no one—not even the hardy and deadly feldragons—came to aid the massive beast in the center of the carnage. No one dared tend his wounds until he was completely free of the monster—for a berserker killed indiscriminately, not differentiating between friend and foe. And Set Tyrne was a berserker like none other ever known.

In a few moon cycles, she would know the feel of those teeth and claws. She crouched down and examined the marvel of shifting death.

He was invulnerable until his magic exhausted itself and he slipped back into feldragon or human skin. However, when he did turn into one of his normal forms, he was as vulnerable as any other extraordinary feldragon warrior.

She reached out a finger to see how long he had left in his berserking state. Her finger passed through him with only the faintest flicker of emotional transference.

Battle lust overwhelmed his emotional landscape at first, but loathing followed by apathy dominated as he regained his human mind for his own.

She cocked her head at that unexpected result. Interesting.

Did he regret the casualties he caused on the battle field? Would he regret being the instrument of her death?

Previous tenders had been dispatched in many ways—all quite permanently. While separated only by a thin shield of unbreakable magic, she had seen Set Tyrne rage. She knew why the leykeepers had decided her fate to be his.

Once a berserker caught a hunting scent, it would follow it to termination.

And there was nothing that a tender could possibly do, of course—especially from a prison so far away.

She smiled. The leykeepers, for all their planning and power and complete control over the dome, never quite understood the sentient power of the garden. And being quite content in their hold over her, they had doubled her usual access to magic.

Whether tenders in the past hadn't understood the magic they could harness, or they hadn't given themselves over to the vines completely, absorbing their knowledge and trust, she didn't know. All that mattered was that she had.

She hadn't possessed the ability to control magic before entering the garden, so she'd absorbed the specific powers like a treesponge when the opportunity had arisen. The vines had whispered ways to wield the darker magics of the garden long ago.

She looked at the beast of nightmares as he slowly turned into a feldragon, then a man, alone on a field.

Her hand accidentally brushed his again, and though there was no tactile sense, again she felt a strange cauldron of emotion.

She considered the beast, weighing options, then pulled a hand through the "air"—sending the water of the pool rippling around her—and called up images of the past.

The view closed in on the feldragons' castles in the trees—marvelous structures built from stone and dark jewels—held in the glittering red boughs of the fiery, unbreakable mangough trees. A perfect habitat for a dragon and cat mix. A tree limb curled and showers of flames erupted from the newly exposed branch tips, reflecting on the onyx and dark crystal stones in a mix of shadow and flame.

More than one species served the feldragons, exchanging autonomy for power and protection, as they skittered, loped, or flew through the trees in brilliant displays of color or sinuous skill to deliver supplies, communications, and completed tasks. The massive jungle around the Southeastern Ley and the caves of the North buffeted the Eastern kingdom, combining multiple habitats for the feldragons to rule.

The memory-water rippled along the castle walks that connected tree bridges between each manse—a dizzying death drop for any being not graceful enough—or with flight powers—to navigate should one slip.

A peril she knew well.

The scene blinked to one of the feldragon revels, where violence, earthy passion, and sensual delight mixed together in the dances on the forest floor, in the boughs of the mangough trees, and along the stone walks.

The feldragons were a dynamic and passionate people that were exciting to watch, but there was only one she sought, and the land's memories moved her to where Set Tyrne sat drinking felmer draught in human form. Under the moonlight, the gleaming silver of his numerous magical scars only served to highlight the threat of the man—of the warrior and ultimate survivor barely concealed beneath rich garments. Overly jeweled women and half-beasts approached him in a combination of poorly hidden fear and excitement.

Set took a slow drink, then a vicious grin appeared on his face, and black scales suddenly rippled up and along his tan, exposed forearms. Silvered battle scars gleamed in warning. He snapped his teeth and the women scattered.

Twenty breaths later, when the eyes of the revel were focused on other things once more, the scales retreated. His head fell back against the stone tree and he looked up into the bejeweled night sky peeking through the eyelet openings in the tree tops. Apathy was the only thing that existed in his gaze. Completely removed from the rest of the revelers, he distanced himself as the celebrants writhed around the boughs.

Lirah's hand stayed for a moment on the image, unable to pull away. Unlike the sapfoxling child, who desperately wanted to belong but could not, Set Tyrne deliberately kept himself away.

Still, there was something there that reminded her of...

Lirah pulled a hand through the watered air of memories, flipping to another. To a charcoal and tan stone manse far to the east, separated from all the rest. There was no bridge used to enter the prohibitive dwelling, and there was little welcome in the doorway or windows facing the impressive expanse of the feldragons' stone and leaf domain to its west. It stood as a lonely, fortified tower at the edge of the warlike decadence of the feldragons' central city.

To its favor, the isolated residence held a breathtaking view on its eastern side. Rolling hills, deadly lakes, glittering forests and sharp mountains stretched for millions of paces.

It was the first and last stand for the feldragons—a timberland stone tower domain hovering high above another world.

The living monument to a beast.

He was lounging inside the tower, again in human form, the back of his head leaning against the frame of an open window, jaded eyes watching two men pace his floor. The men, though obviously angry, carefully maintained their distance. In their human forms the three looked remarkably similar—the resemblance of the king, crown prince, and second prince was strong, even with the multitude of scars the second prince wore in silvered lines upon his skin.

An exalted, but lonely existence—the weapon that all revered and feared—the brutal savior of his people, so brutal that not even his own kin approached without fear.

To be surrounded, yet always alone.

The vines tightened at the turn of her thoughts, rippling the aired memories in their agitation.

With us, sister, with us, never alone.

"Shhh, I know." She stroked the ones crawling up her sides. "I was thinking of before."

Before, before, doesn't matter.

The memories dissolved and she was back on the battlefield.

Childlike in their understanding, the vines curled in her arms. She stroked them again as she considered the beast collapsed in the obliterated field.

Alone.

The image rippled—the vines of the dome that hadn't already gathered around her now slithered along the surface of the pond and wrapped around her limbs, showing themselves in the reflection of the magic she was using to ghost walk.

You have us, sister. They whispered with the slides of their bodies and the pluck of their envenomed tips along her sleeves. You always will.

She smoothed a hand along their green flesh and looked at the current image—at the beast whose monstrous scales were slowly receding. In three lunar cycles' time, magic would call him to the dome in berserking form, the leykeepers would lift the barriers, and he would enter to deliver her death.

But now, he was alone on the field. Abandoned by his brethren prior to his decisive victory. An invulnerable creature that would turn into a man with a susceptible human body.

A vulnerable time for an otherwise immortal beast.

Her palm touched the image of the ground, sending magic from the interior circle of the garden to the Northeastern Ley. In the real field, an unattached vine slipped from the timberline and slithered toward the monster—ignoring the large, invisible barrier of space that naturally surrounded him, even when he was in a room with his family.

It was a hard truth never to approach a berserker still partially in form—a law of the land akin to how things were sucked into the sky and ripped apart during a tornadic wind. Unlike the archers, though, she was undetectable in her present state.

The vine continued, for Lirah had an advantage that the leykeepers hadn't foreseen her using. With the extra magic that she had been given for this moon's cycle, and the vines happy to do her bidding in anything except sidestepping her own sacrifice, she could do anything she wanted to their uncontrollable pet in this moment.

Even kill him.

The deadly vine moved over him, unfurling as it flowed until its venom-bloated tip touched the heavy, bloodied scales that were receding over his heart. It would be so easy, to wipe away the threat.

She had possessed little choice in life, but she had choice in this.

The venomous tip swelled, waiting for her direction. She stared down at him for long moments, then unfurled her fingers. At the signal, the tip burst outward into crystal petals of blush and gold. A stamen teardrop fell and healing magic seeped between the receding scales of the beast.

Chapter Three:
Dance of the Vines

Lirah tended the garden in the dusk-rise of the moon's quarter rise. She spent nearly every waking moment in service to the plants, flowers, and bubbles of magic that served the garden and Nexus, but each quarter cycle of the moon was special.

Green and purple vines danced and sliced through the air in anticipation of the Quarter Draw, flowers bloomed in a riotous mass of color and movement, and the iridescent bubbles popped as they were snapped from the air. The activity created a natural melody in the dome as the living flora bent in their generated breeze and rubbed their disparate textures together.

The purple vines weaved a slower dance than their green counterparts. They had become fat with glut—the used magic that they sucked in was near to bursting, needing the release of the conversion that occurred on each quarter turn of the moon.

At her signal, the purple vines connected to the eight ley lines for one final pull. They sucked in the dregs of the dead and twisted magic that pulsed through the kingdoms, then detached and sluggishly slithered to the Nexus.

The green vines swayed violently on their leafy feet and the hum of the dome's magic increased.

Surrounded by the revelry on all sides, Lirah stepped onto the very center of the Nexus—the point where all leys connected. She raised her arms with palms extended upward, and let the crescendo of the dance commence. The red tips of the purple vines descended, crimson lightning split the air and her skin. Strike, strike, strike, they injected death into her veins.

The venom spread between one flash and the next, constricting her veins in sharp, excruciating waves. She held still, arms out.

Long practice had taught her how to deal with the pain.

As the venom raced toward her heart, the mint-tipped vines fluidly moved between their companions. Strike, strike, strike, they made their own strikes upon her skin, pulling the venom free.

The physical relief of having the venom removed made her lightheaded and she swayed with the vines, letting their mesmeric dance take her too—the vessel that facilitated the exchange, renewing the magic between old and new.

The green vines connected to the ley lines and injected the newly minted magic into the veins of the land.

Strike. Consume. Exchange. Consume. Release.

They transformed the used and twisted magic back into that which aided the transformation and renewal of the other living beings in the kingdoms.

The magic pulsed out as each draw made it cleaner and stronger, giving the glorious creatures of their world speed, power, and metamorphosis—strengthening the glistening wings of the butterfly people, unfurling the fierce leathery veins of the dragon people, giving all of them the magic that allowed a long, full life.

As a result of this quarterly exchange, aging had slowed in the last two decades across all species that lived within the leys, and had halted senescence nearly completely over the last five. The supposition was that those born now would experience three hundred years of flush health.

Lirah would live to eighteen.

She looked at her skin, rotating one arm to look at the flesh beneath as the dance continued. The celadon hue was growing stronger, the plants changing her a bit more each week the dance commenced. Her eyes, reflected in the garden pool, were turning viridian. A small smile grew. She was indeed being changed.

It was during the garden's coda—the vines growing lethargic and falling one-by-one in a transfixed daze—that the exterior ley circle vibrated in warning. Lirah jerked her head to look through the barrier of the dome and into the foliage surrounding the exterior grove. Vines released from service—sisters to the ones inside the dome—always gathered outside during a Quarter Draw, waving in memory of the magical dance their younger brethren within the dome were engaged in.

The elder, released vines did not have the active deadliness of the vines still in service to the garden, but they were often...hungry. And they didn't distinguish prey based on species.

She had never seen anyone try to navigate their tightly weaving assembly. Whatever approached was either incredibly foolish, or incredibly dangerous.

As the bushes parted, Lirah drew in a sharp breath. A feldragon larger than normal walked the Northeastern Ley, magic sparking around it.

It was a very specific and distinct black feldragon—a feldragon who never visited the dome in this form, where he was intelligent and aware.

Lirah's throat felt oddly dry as she watched the black, saber-toothed dragon prowl closer.

Showing no hesitation, he proceeded painfully through the electrified barrier and approached the very edge of the dome, staring hard inside. The vines weaved around him expectantly—oddly waiting. One stroked a black scale and a bead of magic glistened—the vine stirring the fading memory of the crystal remnant.

He bared his teeth at the touch, but didn't break the gaze he held on her, a gaze that held none of the empty or jaded expression that she usually observed in the looking glass. He was sharp, focused, and actively annoyed.

Heart pounding, Lirah walked forward and tilted her head, not breaking the connected gaze.

There were many creatures and beings that were curious about the garden, the dome, the magic, and the lone creature that existed to tend its center. They roamed the grove around the dome constantly on any night other than a Quarter Draw. However, even on a normal evening, they never drew close enough to broach the electrified field encompassing the ley circles, for the pain was excruciating. Not even those who came in prayer passed the lines. She'd seen people she once knew trying to shout to be heard, but they had needed to stand too far away for even lip reading. The leykeepers actively prevented anyone from communicating or drawing near through the pain of the process, and threatened death if convicted.

The only exception to this was the bait trail the leykeepers had strewn for the berserker.

But though he had raged in his beastly form around the edges of the grove during the past few cycles—he had never visited the grove in one of his two more rational forms.

On four clawed paws, he stepped back to the edge of the exterior ley circle without breaking her gaze.

Lirah's heart was beating so hard that the plants had begun to regather around her—even the vines that were too drunk on magic to fully rise flopped a pace closer.

The feldragon's eyes narrowed on one of the vines reaching up toward her, then he looked down at the ley circle. He walked around it, pushing the exterior vines out of the way as if they weren't venomous, man-eating stalks, and examined each of the small discs that designated the intersections of the ley rays with the exterior circle.

Unable to stop the automatic movement of her feet, she mirrored his path within the interior circle, keeping him in front of her at all times so she could watch him. Stepping past the exterior circle was an action punishable by death. Other than the leykeepers, this was the most interaction she had had with anyone in seventy moons' time.

He padded over each ley ray and joining circle, looking for something. Still in feldragon form, he sniffed the Northeastern Ley again. His sharp gaze rose back to her. His regard was calculating and fierce, unlike his regular apathy or berserking glaze, and such a look had never been focused on her.

She swallowed oddly again, uncertain why her throat was so dry.

His feldragon scales—less deadly than those of his berserking form, but still brilliantly fierce elements of nature—rippled. An object moved along the path, riffling out, then fell to the moss growing alongside the Northeastern Ley.

He bared his long sharp teeth, snapped at her in warning, then bounded off into the forest, heedless of the pain from crossing the ley circle again.

A cracked crystal glinted on the moonlit moss where he had stood.

With her hand upon her chest, Lirah stood still for so long that the moon had long risen before she gave into the increasingly worried cries of the vines and withdrew to the center of the dome.

Her fingers were already reaching for the water.

Chapter Four: A Gift of Tears

At the highest point of the sun on the following day, when his scarred body was once more splayed upon a bloodied field, another vine unfurled its poisoned tip to drop a healing crystal upon his chest.

And Lirah waited.

When he reappeared outside the dome that nightfall, a foreign sensation vibrated through her.

The large feldragon snapped his teeth and slammed the second crystal to the ground before disappearing into the brush.

Heart in her throat, the vines wrapped around her in distress and confusion.

Why are you smiling like that, sister, when your chest beats so? They called.

She shook her head and ran to the pond waters to watch his retreat as he angrily soared through the star-filled sky.

She sent a third crystal. Then a fourth, fifth, tenth—issuing more healing magic with each gift.

Each was returned with a vicious snap of saber teeth and whip of a spade tail.

Returned to her, and he had to cut through the ley circle each time to do so. With each return, his deadly feldragon jaws came increasingly closer to the edges of the unbreakable dome—closer contact to her than any rationally minded being in the previous seventy moons' time had dared. For when he visited in his larger berserker form, he was without reason, and was more akin to the battering of a devastating wind—soulless, unknowing, and without mercy.

But in this form, with glittering, intelligent eyes that spoke of anger, outrage, and warning, she wanted him closer still. It became an addiction for her.

Healing balms changed to tokens. Tokens became small items of comfort. And each was returned by him personally, viciously left on the moss between the leys. Her last gift had been especially brash, too—a crystal formed into the shape of one of the felroses that climbed the lower walls of his lonely stone fortress.

Even she didn't know her reasoning for that—she'd only known that it had made her heart beat triple to do it.

The addiction was becoming something more.

Lirah's eyes moved to the brush surrounding the Northeastern Ley. She could feel him coming. Anticipation sharpened within her.

The animals in the forest surrounding the grove shifted with unease, but didn't take flight, which was unusual. Her heart picked up additional speed. This was not a response to a feldragon appearing in their midst.

The bushes parted, a large form emerged from the trees, and her breath caught. The form wasn't of a berserker or a feldragon.

The powerfully built human drew closer with smooth, prowling steps. A predatory animal in any form, Set Tyrne's build was not hulking, yet every lean muscle group exhibited its use for survival in the purest sense. He was sculpted like a predator, powerful even in human skin.

An apex killer in his most unsettling form.

Indigo eyes contained the barest hint of violet, and they didn't twitch as he stepped through the second electrified net. She could see the muscles in his shoulders tense as they accommodated the pain.

He stopped at the edge of the dome, so close, and flicked the crystal rose in his fingers at it. He said something as the dome's magic pulsed and threw the rose back at his feet—but sound couldn't pierce the dome's magic, even this close, and the skipping of her heart and overwhelming sensory details she was taking in wouldn't let her understand what his lips were demanding of her.

She shook her head slowly, her entire body picking up the furious tempo of her chest along with a heightened sense of something.

Intelligent eyes focused on the dome, the leys, the circles—his gaze assessed everything. He lifted the rose he had cast away, then strode over and dropped it on the Northeastern Leypoint—on the circle point where the Northeastern Leykeeper usually set his amulet.

"Why?" Set's voice was rough and dominant, clearly demanding she answer.

Rocked at the sound, she blindly gripped one of the gnarled, leafless trees that had grown to support the vines. A vine crawling there twined over her hand, peeling her fingers away so it could twine over her shaking palm.

She gripped the vine and curled it against her chest, where her heart thumped furiously.

"Of what"—she cleared her suddenly dry throat—"do you wish to know?"

"Why do you give the beast a flower?" he asked harshly.

It confirmed many things she had begun to suspect—that he wasn't one with his berserking nature, and more importantly, that he had no desire to be.

"What difference does it make why?"

"You will tell me." Dark threats were deep in each single syllable.

"Will I?" Her heart didn't slow, even as she caught her bearings. He was no leykeeper to threaten her.

"If you value—"

"There is little that you can do to me, Prince. Not while I'm in this cage." The approach of death, and the lack of presence of the leykeepers, brought a subversive freedom to her speech.

"You won't always be inside your enclosure."

"And you won't always be without it."

Pointed, deadly tips grew from his fingers. "You will be naught but a streak of red upon my claws."

She smiled. "As it is willed and fated."

He narrowed his eyes. "Whatever game you think might spare you, you have failed already. The beast has your scent. You gave it to him further with your meaningless gifts."

"You have raged here in that form countless times as is."

"From the leykeepers baiting him to the magic. Not to you."

"When the magic falls, I will meet the same end, whether your beast cares or not."

"You are a foolish girl if you think one end similar to another."

"Foolish? It is punishable by death to even be where you are standing."

She wanted to take the words back as soon as she said them.

He smiled a feral grin. Human teeth glistened with a promise of something far sharper. "Who will move me or deal such a blow?"

Vines wrapped up her legs in response to her relief. She pulled another against her chest. He was still speaking—still standing there instead of flying into the night. Her heart continued to beat a rhythm triple to the faded memory of a morning birdsong she had once loved.

His gaze followed the vines wrapping around her. "Your venomous plants?" he scoffed, motioning at the twining vines and misinterpreting their motions. "They keep giving me gifts."

"They can do much worse," she snapped in response, regretting it again. Why was she responding like this? She was the Tender of the Garden—calm, serene, above petty emotion.

"Let them." He paced aggressively on human legs, gaze never leaving hers. "Or maybe you think a leykeeper up to the task of moving me? A weak priest who has to use an amulet to speak through the Nexus's magic?"

She looked at the rose sitting on the ley point. If the leykeepers knew that someone without an amulet could speak to her in such a way...? If she had known...?

She shook her head. Who would she have enlisted to speak?

She stroked the vine in her arms, trying to calm her emotions. She was tranquil. Serene. The epitome of the vestal Tender of the Garden. "The leykeepers highly discourage anyone who attempts contact."

"Spreading their blood would be worth the laugh. And who else will move me? All but the leykeepers are forbidden to speak to or approach you."

And yet, knowing this, here he was, still speaking—speaking to her.

More vines wrapped her legs, confused by the hammering sound in her chest—wondering what could have produced this emotion that wasn't fear.

"These are the vines that are so feared?" He sneered. "The ones that cling to you like weak children?"

"Do not doubt their power." Her mind couldn't grab a direction, helpless to know what to say to keep him there. She had been so long without conversation that didn't involve formal speech that responding in any normal way to prolong communication seemed beyond her.

"I don't think it is I who should be worried about their power," he said, sharp grin on his full lips as he looked at the green and purplish-red vines. "Your children they might be now, but they will consume you in the end. Are you frightened, Little Tender? To be torn apart?"

"I do not fear my end."

In two cycles more, there would be another girl, somewhere in the kingdoms, pricked by a thorn, then bleeding gold; tested and confirmed as the next tender. And a moon cycle after that...Lirah would finally transform, on the altar of grass. Bleeding out the remnants of gold that infused her blood and returning the magic to cultivate the Nexus for the next cycle.

She did not fear her end, but if she had one regret, it was for the next tender.

The vines wrapped around her in agitation and despair. Are we not your companions? Do you not love us?

"Of course I do," she murmured. But it was a whisper to the wind, for the vines communicated in a manner that was not human, and her mind interpreted their words for her own.

It was both rich and fulfilling, and a terribly lonely existence to live inside the dome. She looked at the gaffer vines twining together, working in harmony—a concordance of beauty and spirit. The tripled patter of her heart slowed to a steadier, aching beat. Soon. Soon she would join them.

Set's gaze, unbelievably, narrowed in on her further. As if there had been some small amount of his attention that hadn't been on her before, and now she was his sole focus.

She stroked the vines, feeling lightheaded. Being the focus of such intensity was a disconcerting, heady feeling.

"Is that why you give gifts to the beast?" he demanded. "Hoping he will make your last moments quick?"

"No." She kept her gaze connected to his. "I seek merely to give you solace in a moment that you are without."

If he had a tail at the moment, it would be whipping side to side in agitation. His full lips thinned.

"I do not require solace. And he requires nothing."

"Then the gifts should barely trouble your thoughts."

Fury overtook his features—and if she were outside the dome, it was likely her death would have come sooner than planned.

His features slid into feldragon form, then he was gone—only the whip of a spade tail to mark his full transformation and flight.

She stared at the spot where he'd stood until the vines physically moved her to the soft moss of her bed. Staring up at the dome, she wondered at the dancing beat in the hollow of her chest.

~*~

She worked nimble fingers through the mirrored pool each day, watching him and working.

If he had thought his visit would cause her actions to cease, it had only increased her attempts. Each time he received a wound, she provided a magic elixir. Each time an arrow strayed too near, a vine leaped to throw it off course. Each time he collapsed, panting in overspent exhaustion, she warmed the moss beneath his scales and skin.

After caustic fights with the King, boundary skirmishes involving wounds mortal to anyone else, and two attempted poisonings, she overwhelmed him with the magic a close companion-at-arms would gift another—gifts he never received otherwise, for everyone knew the beast needed nothing of comfort or healing.

Crystals were dropped near his curled fingers when he was abnormally weary, and healing balms placed upon his chest post-battle. His reactions never disappointed—and he continued to pace and snarl in warning in front of the dome.

But he also stopped staring jadedly into the distance when he was alone. He spent his free moments now actively focused and brimming with murderous intent. Irritated and snapping, and without any of the indifference he had exhibited before.

There was no apathy in what she was coaxing from him.

It became a craving more than a game. She healed him, comforted him when he was barely conscious, and poked at the caustic shadows surrounding him whenever someone would flee from his snapping jaws at a revel.

With each interference, he grew angrier and more alive—more animated as he raged at her in human form—and threw the husks of gifted magic to the ground. But his responses only served her resolve.

And when the trance blooms saturated the air around the grove between the quarter cycles, he transformed into the beast of nightmares, and she watched him rage and tear, bearing witness to another part of him—one that overrode his tight control. The creature that would be her doom.

She paced the beast on the interior of the dome, letting her fingers drag through the thorn plants that populated the edges of the garden. Every living creature within a thousand paces had fled as soon as the trance blooms had burst. Everything in the Cruel Lands knew the smell of the trance honey upon the air and what it wrought.

Set Tyrne in berserking form. A magnificent creature—uncontrollable and savage—straight out of the nightmare of a Second Layer mage. Brutal and vicious, the ultimate weapon of his people, protecting their borders and safety, but never ever to be approached, not even in feldragon or human form.

She touched the thorns of a vine, letting the tip of the stalk twine in her palm, and watched him wear himself out.

When he was done and sprawled upon the grass, she stepped to the very edge of the interior ley circle and put a hand on the cold metal ray nearest to him. It warmed immediately beneath her hand and a tiny amount of the magic she had been allotted shot out to the outer ley circle, spreading and warming the grass. It took little magic to reach out the few paces from the dome where he had fallen.

A tiny crystal formed upon his outstretched palm. He gripped the offering and crushed the crystal against the leypoint nearest him.

"Stop this silliness," he said harshly, staring at the sky.

"No."

"What do you want? Why use magic on a beast that has no need of your gesture? Why waste it on the softening of wounds that will eventually heal on their own? Why stop scars that would simply be one of many? Why do you not try to end the monster that will end you?"

She knelt next to the edge of the dome, simple paces away from his outstretched form, and folded her legs beneath her. "I considered it."

He gave a harsh laugh and finally looked over, dark indigo gaze meeting hers. "Then rabbit-moused away like the scared little human you are?"

"Consideration is the asking of a question and the contemplation of an answer. What good would it do for me to end your life?" she asked quietly.

"What good does it do for you to save it? For I will kill you."

"It is my fate to be ended upon your claws," she said.

He sneered. "More likely at this point upon my teeth."

"That is certainly possible."

"You are a stupid girl."

She spread her fingers into the moss at her sides. "And yet, even the stupid can use their allotted magic as they wish."

Anger curled his mouth, but she had traded insults with him often enough to know he wouldn't bolt—and that if he did, he'd be back.

Whatever he saw in her expression, made his more furious. "You will stop this game, Tender, or I will make your end so horrifying that you will scream to the winds for release."

She let the vines curl around her. To someone else, it might look like a protective gesture, but they were excited about this possibility.

The more blood, the better. You will join us all the quicker.

"It doesn't matter what your pets think they might do to help you," he said, sneering. "I'll kill them too."

"No," she said. "The vines will help, not hinder you in your task. Do not harm them."

His eyes narrowed on the vines as they curled, winding around her, then focused back upon her with a new, calculating look to his gaze.

"You are a sad girl who has forgotten what it is to be free."

"Perhaps that is why I'm drawn to you," she said, tilting her head. "I see someone who understands."

Death looked her in the eyes—apathy was the absolute last thing reflected in his gaze now—and she nodded at the emotions she saw there. A strange satisfaction touched the dwindling hollow within her.

"Do as you will, Set Tyrne, Dark Prince of the Cruel Lands, and so too will I."

Chapter Five: To Be Seen

The garden's magic stores increased further with each rise of the moon, as the garden readied for the end of one act and the beginning of the next. Lirah stopped passively watching the kingdoms at large and instead actively took part in proceedings closer to her heart—allocating her extra magic to aid Set and provide distant companionship to the sapfoxling child.

Having finished checking in on the girl for the day—making the vines dance for her and chasing away any children with ill intentions—Lirah entered the pond.

Wrapped in water, she unfurled upon a grassy plain in the southwest—an invisible specter upon the field as always, able to view, but unable to interact.

As soon as she came within range of Set, though, sound suddenly bloomed. She nearly lost the hold on her watery cloak, as she froze in awe.

The magic of the garden's pool made it so that she could see, but she could not hear, taste, smell, or touch. She'd learned to lip-read while gazing through the pool, but had never achieved true audition. She touched the cloak of water to her ears and held back tears. If the leykeepers had hinted to this at any point, she would have eagerly anticipated it.

The sounds grew as she approached her target, making her stride to reach him all the more quickly.

Set was standing by himself on the ridge, in human form, staring down at the raging battle.

Lirah liked to stand beside him, even though she was unseen—to watch him and be ready to give aid. There was always satisfaction in giving aid quickly, for it vexed him immensely—not knowing how it was done.

"What are you doing, Tender?"

She temporarily lost hold of the magic wrapped around her, and only sheer desperation pulled it back together, grounding her in place. "What...you...you can see me?"

He looked directly at her, tearing his gaze away from the battle. "Are you so witless that I need question your ability to understand speech now too?"

"But no one can see me during a waterwalk." She stumbled back to look at the group of military officers standing a short distance away. They were near enough that she should be noticed, yet all of them remained focused on the battle.

Set bared his teeth. "A what? A living nightmare intended solely for me then. I'm so pleased."

No one else could see her, but if Set could, then maybe...

She reached out to touch him, and though he flinched away from her—as if her fingers would connect—her hand sliced through his image.

She curled her fingers into a fist. She hadn't touched another human's skin in more than seventy full cycles of the moon. It had been a vain hope.

"What are you doing, Tender?" he repeated, voice sharper.

"Witnessing your day," she said, looking back to the battle and pretending that he wasn't asking something else.

"Don't you have duties to attend? Or is the eleventh Tender of the Garden beginning to laze about in her final full moons?"

"I never avoid my duties," she said, voice a bit sharp. "The garden is at rest."

"How lovely. You get to rest soon, as well. I do hope you are looking forward to it."

The sneering normality made her relax.

"You are a terrible conversationalist," she said, still too moved by the fact that she was actually having a conversation to be bothered by its deficiencies.

"You aren't the nectar of a peachfruit either," he snapped.

"I guess we both require practice." She smiled.

His gaze moved to her lifting lips and hackles rippled along his back, before disappearing back into human skin. "You are mistaken for thinking I care."

She tilted her head. "Is happiness unnerving to you? Should I smile more?" She tried another smile, this one less natural. She wasn't used to smiling. The tender was all things stately, graceful, and mysterious. It would be no comfort to the kingdoms if she were to smile at everyone.

This time he just stared at her balefully. "That's not a smile." He bared his teeth at her.

"Neither is that," she said pointedly.

"It's the smile of death."

"More so the grimace of death, I think."

"I didn't realize that was one of your tasks," he enunciated. "Thinking."

"Yours either." She nodded. "We have both learned something today."

"Go away, Tender. Back to your flock."

She withheld a smile with force and calmly responded with, "I unnerve you so much?"

He bared his teeth again. "I find a gnat unnerving only in the time it takes me to squash it."

She looked over to where his compatriots were hunkered down—some in human form, some as feldragons. "They stay far from you."

"As I wish it."

"Does no one speak to you?"

"As I wish it." He was looking at her with an uncomplimentary expression.

She let her gaze roam his face—tracing his strong and ruthless features with her eyes—the actions of the battle receding to the background of her view. "Your loneliness is keen. And you know not how to overcome it."

"You put your own feelings on me," he said savagely. "Do not."

She looked off to the battle, the happiness from before fading back to contemplative calm. "Perhaps, that is what I'm doing. A little."

At the admission, she could feel the vines coiling around her back in the garden's pool, and she spared a bit of calm for them.

"Fifty breaths more," a voice said.

She looked sharply to the side to see a feldragon officer addressing Set. There was a slice of apprehension in the officer's voice that he couldn't contain.

"I can hear him," she murmured.

"Good for you," Set said to her with a sneer.

The officer took a few quick steps back.

"They fear you," she said, speaking her thoughts aloud still, for the sheer novelty of it.

"As they should." He closed his eyes and stretched his neck in a slow circle, readying himself to transform. "Leave."

"Yes, Prince," the officer said, backing away more quickly now. But Set wasn't even paying attention to the man who was obeying a command not meant for him.

Lirah paid little attention to the fleeing officer either; her eyes focused on the way Set stretched, long muscles pulling.

"Does it hurt?" she asked.

"It is like fire burning through each vein," he said in a tone that suddenly seemed tired. "I've grown long used to it."

She focused magic through the leys and a yellow flower bloomed at his feet. At its appearance, he snapped out of his fatigue and crushed it with his heel.

"But you," he said, the grinding motions of his foot mashing the petals into pulp. "Will feel that agony as a fresh pain with every last breath you take."

The healing fluids from the flower seeped into his skin with the destruction of its shell, and she smirked as he swore.

"Meddlesome, stupid, interfering—"

"It is time," the same officer called, the apprehension of the group accelerating as they watched their greatest warrior pulverize a flower, then swear at it.

She smiled fiendishly and made another one bloom. He crushed that one, too, giving her a look that was so foul and full of death that her smile widened into a stupidly large grin.

"I will kill you," he promised.

"I know," she said, and grew two more.

The officers could only hear Set, though, and it was amusing to see apex predators looking so spooked. "Er...right, ready on my signal," the officer ordered.

The soldiers who were still in human form transformed immediately and shifted their weight to the front pads of their taloned paws, awaiting their commander's signal.

Only the top ranking officer—a general—remained in human form to order the transition. His fingers shook as he placed a small horn in his mouth. Set sneered at him before returning his gaze to the battlefield, muscles tensing in anticipation.

As soon as the horn blew, the feldragon officers launched into the air. Below, the infantry feldragons and their serving beasts on the field acknowledged the alert. Some fled to the edges of the battlefield; others took flight to keep the enemy corralled. As quickly as their limbs would take them, everyone abandoned the area that Set would first reach.

"Leave," Set said to her.

"In a moment, Your Highness," the general responded, gripping the horn with shaking fingers. "I need to witness the formation to make certain th—"

Set sneered without looking at the man, and even though Set's gaze remained on Lirah, and far from the general, the man swallowed heavily.

"Leave," Set repeated to her.

"I can witness from the air," the general said, throwing himself into transformation. He took straight to the skies like cannon shot, automatically maneuvering against the possible swipe of transitioning berserker claws that had gutted feldragons before him.

"Leave." Set ordered again, his voice becoming a growl. He viciously pulled a vial from his pocket, decapitated the cap, then held it beneath his nose.

The shape of the battle was changing even as he did so—the feldragons losing ground immediately as they loosely penned in their foes instead of actively fighting them. The tide of the battle would change again in ten breaths more.

"No. I will stay here with you. I will be here through the change," Lirah said to Set.

"I don't want you here." His voice was half-human, half the roar of the beast as he crushed the glass and swiped at her.

Even in a waterwalk as strange as today's, she couldn't smell the odor seeping from the crushed trance flowers, but she knew the scent well. The flowers had bloomed in the western villages, but it was nothing compared to the strength which the garden produced every midpoint between a dance. The vapor smelled honeysuckle sweet and ferrous sharp.

She had witnessed his change from afar before and it was a painful and beautiful transition observed by few who were still living. He was terrifying and glorious in transformation as his skin and bones broke and reformed. It was nothing like the smooth, painless transition from human to feldragon. His transformation into the beast was as vicious and painful as the being he transformed into.

As the change overtook him, she released bursts of white flowers from the balm clover surrounding him. Each brushed petal would bring him relief from the ensuing pain.

He gritted his teeth and roared at her, but she could see the clover doing its work. His roar was one of anger, not pain.

And then the beast stood in his place. There was no reflection of anger or identification there—he knew her not at all in this form—but in this skin, too, he could see her on the field. He launched himself in a move far too quick for a predator of his size and sliced through her. The claw blades carved harmlessly through her image. Then he was off like a deadly strike of lightning as the sounds and smells of the ongoing battle captured the beast's complete attention.

She shadowed him through the battleground and watched the carnage—watched her fate play out before her. But when the battlefield was bathed in blood and the beast had fallen to regain his previous form, she knelt by his side and healed him. And before releasing her watery cloak, she made another patch of clover bloom beneath.

Chapter Six: Reverence and Cruelty

"How did you do it?" he asked, once more in human form, as he angrily paced the exterior ley circle as the sun rose.

"Do what?" she asked negligently, trying to control the constant thrill that took hold of her each time he emerged from the forest.

"Stand next to me before the battle."

"Before the battle only? Not during? I walked the whole way with you during your transformed state."

He snapped his teeth. "And still you stand there, calm and unconcerned. Immune. Safe inside your cage, you do not understand your need to be terrified."

Her heart was beating far too fast for anyone to claim calm, but it wasn't from fear. It wasn't like when the elders had dropped her from the boughs of the trees when she was seven to see if terror would make her fly. The bones in her body had only fully healed once she'd experienced five of the leeching and renewing rituals in the garden. But she could still feel the agonizing limp she'd carried for five years, and the broken bits in her spine, like a phantom pain, born of terror.

No, it wasn't fear she felt when she looked upon him.

"Perhaps I simply marvel at the magnificence of your form."

His pacing grew more erratic. "You wouldn't survive a day outside. How you even made it twelve summers to be chosen as tender is beyond my ability to comprehend."

In her youth she had carried endless buckets for washing, scrubbed infinite pots for cooking, and sharpened interminable amounts of tools, all while keeping her head down, her chipped back to the cave walls, and her eyes moving. She'd barely left the caves after her clan had determined she would never fly or prowl—that's how she had survived in a world where she was solely prey.

She touched the edge of the dome, letting the magic vibrate across her skin.

He followed the motion. "You are trapped in there. How did you follow me?"

"I know not how the magic works." A partial truth.

"I have never heard of a tender being seen outside the confines of her prison."

"It's not a prison," she said softly. "And perhaps no other has used their extra allotment in this way."

"Allotment?" His eyes narrowed.

"For my service." She tipped her head.

His intent look transformed and a cruel smile curved his lips. "Is that what the leykeepers told you? That by the grace of their goodwill and your excellent service, that you are gifted with this magic? They are liars and thieves."

Too late, she realized she should have said nothing. She had never needed to worry about keeping secrets—for she had no one to share secrets with.

"You think the magic rises on its own." She didn't answer the obvious trap in his words. She could see the truth in his eyes—or at least the truth as he saw it. "That it is part of the natural cycle. That the leykeepers can't control its measure."

"Of course. What are they but empty mouthpieces that control an amulet and a tradition? But you, you wish to be so blessed, don't you?"

It was a direct hit and she couldn't stop herself from showing it. "Far better to believe myself blessed then mislead."

He smiled cruelly. "A sheep that requires prepping for slaughter."

"And you, the weapon. Revered."

"An interesting word. I see the desire in your eyes. I visited your tribe three sunrises ago," he said, prowling the edge of the dome, a glint in his eyes that spoke of nothing good.

She raised her chin. "Then you saw that they know what I've done. Two hundred and ninety two quarter moons of unbroken service." She planted her feet. "Galeria Shyn claimed only five more than that. I will surpass her record. I will have three hundred when I am finished. I will be the most celebrated tender who has ever lived."

"The Eagliger Tribe finally counted you among their number when you became tender, didn't they? Their defective secret transforming into their golden, sacrificial goose."

She held steady. Anger and despair was for the twenty moon tender she had once been and sadness for the turn of fifty. A Lirah with seventy-plus full moons of service would not allow herself such emotion. She was the best tender this world had seen. She had made it so.

She motioned at the grove. "The landscape is alive with more magic than at any other time in living memory."

"Yes, you've been such a good tender," he crooned. "Passing on the magic to the rest of us. An unchangeling girl serving her betters."

"Your cruel words serve no purpose."

"As do not your little gifts." His tail lashed out—the change half-bleeding over him. "Do not follow me again."

"No?" She thrust both hands at his feet and made an entire garden grow.

Chapter Seven: Control

A series of battles raged across the southeastern rushes over the next week, and she made certain to accompany him to each, using most of her available magic to do so.

The reptilian and insect people to the south were clever enemies looking to extend their reach across the increasingly smaller border of their own lands and into that of the butterflies' Southern Ley slice, the feldragons' vast kingdom further to the east, and all the fertile resources surrounding the Nexus.

"They are tenacious," Lirah said, as she stood by Set's side for the seventh time in as many days.

"You have something in common then," Set said, pacing in agitation.

The beast prowled under his skin as he whipped himself back and forth, the shadow of a tail in the gesture. He was usually far calmer at the precipice of engagement. That he was agitated showed a wariness that was unfamiliar.

He was too used to her shadowing him now for the gesture to be due to her presence. Something was off today.

She looked over the raging battlefield trying to see what had stirred him. She was no tactician, but she'd watched enough battles with Set now to know that the enemy wasn't reacting in the usual way. Their careful, coordinated attacks were baiting, but not fierce, as if they were holding their ground until a better moment. It was a similar strategy to how the feldragons operated right before Set was unleashed.

"The beetles and snakes are cunning, and their size is an advantage," she admitted. "They are faring better than their brethren."

"They are stupid, thinking they have a handle on any fight here."

"And on you?"

"Yes." He bared his human teeth. "Anyone who thinks they have a handle on me deserves their fate."

She cast a glance to the left, where his two brothers stood with their advisers and military tacticians, coordinating the battle from up high, and waiting for the right moment to unleash the weapon they distanced themselves from.

"Why are the other princes here?" They hadn't been present at any of the other battles.

He waved a dismissive hand. "The beetles are proving resistant to our lessons and Xeric thinks it is due to him watching poor recordings from the field rather than any strategic fault of his own. He means to end the conflict by watching directly, then crushing them tomorrow."

The eldest prince was renowned for his fierce mind, cutting temper, and arrogance, so she was hardly surprised Xeric Tyrne might think such a thing. The feldragons were too accustomed to handing their enemies stunning defeats, even without the use of Set.

"Desperation does odd things to people," she said softly. "Your father won't cede the land he took from the insects last year."

"Of course he won't," Set said dismissively. "And we've been steadily destroying them each time they try. Which calls into further question, why are the ground dwellers fighting today?"

"Is today a poorer day to die than the others in the past week?"

"It is a festival day in their central city."

Lirah looked at the battle with new eyes. The sense that the other side was waiting for something to occur sparked unsettled feelings. "You should speak to your brother of this."

"I'm speaking to you, an idiot who can only speak to me in return because she is hidden behind magic even the beast cannot break," he said bitterly.

"You have some control to spare today," she said. "You haven't raged against the dome in three moonlights' time."

"Would it dissuade you from visiting here if I did? What use is it to be angry at the idiot dormouse who forgets the trap in her quest for nuts?"

"It would not dissuade me," she concurred.

More importantly, she wasn't certain if he wanted it to anymore. He'd barely scowled at her arrival today. He was getting used to her.

She knew that unsettled him too.

He'd begun to look upon her offerings with the resigned sort of expression typical to beasts swayed by the full moon—they looked up at it knowing that it would appear every cycle whether they wished it or not.

Set still threw every one of her offerings into the ley network around the dome, but no longer were they crushed upon the metal.

"Nothing short of death is going to dissuade you, idiot human that you are." But the reply was, at best, half-hearted in its vehemence.

"Tell them of your fears."

Violent anger sprang to his eyes. "I fear nothing."

"Everyone fears something," she said quietly. "To ignore it is to be weak."

"Speak not to me of weakness, Tender."

"Speak of strength instead? That you are strong and capable in any form? That you don't need to rely on your third form to win? That you could win with your mind or your physical gift for battle?"

"I'm nothing without the beast."

"You are everything without the beast," she said quietly. "And everything with."

"You speak doubly false."

"I speak a truth you don't wish to hear. You will rule these lands with your brothers one day. You can make them listen to your doubts."

"Doubts of what? Nothing matters in this idiotic skirmish as soon as I turn. I am the Death Knell, the Sword Upon the Field, the Might of the North, the Terror of the East. The lizards and beetles will learn how I earned those names today and be wiped from the world."

"And many more battles will be, and have been, won by the enemy not engaging at all—knowing that the form so feared will be their end, if they do. One day, when you are at peace and in control—"

"Peace? I have control of all that I—"

Surprise ripped across his features and he contorted in agony, transforming from human to raging beast in the blink of a second.

Shocked, Lirah looked around and saw the tiny groundling hiding between the blades of grass. Having slipped past the sentries in his tiniest of forms—that of a golden beetle—he was holding three crushed blooms in one pincer and murmuring sounds of sacrifice and glory.

The manbeetle was the first to fall to the beast he had forced to transform.

The feldragons began shouting and everything moved slowly in her vision as the beast ripped into the officers who always stood apart from Set, but who were far too near for him to change without warning.

And it was the blessing and curse of the berserker to recognize neither friend nor foe in his raging state.

"My Prince!" someone shouted, as the eldest prince—the Crown Prince and Chief Strategist of the Feldragon Council—was speared through the back by long, razor claws.

"My Princes!" yelled another officer as the youngest prince fell next under his brother's claws. "Retreat!"

Two feldragons ran to the fallen princes, and the beast charged toward them, taking Lirah's ability to hear sound with him.

Lirah stood rooted to her spot, witnessing the carnage in strange, eerie silence. Some of the feldragon officers escaped, but others didn't. The reptiles and insects would die today, too, but their plan hadn't been for the warriors of today—it had been for the ones of tomorrow.

Set always triggered the transformation himself on the battlefield precisely for this reason. Once transformed, he held no account of his actions. The control of the transformation itself—other than on the days the leykeepers baited it, or when the mid-quarter turn of the moon and trance flowers demanded it—had always been his.

And it had just been taken from him.

Chapter Eight: Regrets

Lirah didn't see him for two days—his feldragon form fled the Cruel Lands and kingdoms to a place her magic couldn't touch.

When he appeared in the grove on the third day, her relief was so visceral that she stumbled and the vines twined around her asking if she was okay.

A crystal rose was crushed in his palm. Saber-toothed claws breached his human fingertips to curl around the shards, then he opened his palm and flung the remains to the moss.

"You will not tame him. No matter what you try." His lips were tight. "Gifts and emotional violations will not sway him. He understands nothing but the hunt and death. Knows not how to differentiate enemy from friend or even his own kin."

Heartache. She bent on one knee and ran her fingers along the ley his foot was touching and sent a comforting pulse through. She knew that the youngest prince wasn't dead yet, but that he soon would be. And the Crown Prince was looking at a lifetime of physical struggle. "May gold give you solace."

He pulled his body away as if stung. "Solace? I seek none of such weak emotion."

"What do you seek?"

"What do you?" He spit. "You seek to play? To change me? To change the nature of the beast? An unchangeling girl who understands nothing about what it is to transform?"

She swallowed and held her chin high. "And yet as an unchangeling, I lack not the understanding of how to hear and interpret the fables and folktales of your people. Merging with the beast in the Tale of One. Discovering the strength of form in Lacsha's Lament. Seeing the beauty in change in Siima Rue. Flying free in The Crowfrog's Split."

"Tales for children."

"Stories that highlight what is important to our cultures."

"And you? From what culture do you spring, with your thin, useless limbs and unchanging face?"

"Even a dormouse has a use," she said quietly. "And a quest."

"A dormouse falls to all. Easy prey."

"Part of the life that surrounds us."

"Dinner and death—that is what you will be in two turns of the moon, Tender."

She tilted her head, and let calm take her. "That has been my fate for many moons. Your mocking makes it no more, nor less, true."

He paced angrily. "You lack fear only because you are behind that pane of magic."

"Do you wish me to fear you?"

He snapped his teeth at her. "I care not what you fear. I think you too stupid to know when to flee."

She laughed without humor. "Where is there to flee? You have been visiting this grove for far longer than I have actively watched you. There is nowhere to flee, Set Tyrne, nor is it my wish."

He said nothing, angrily moving around the ley circle.

She eyed him, trying to read what was beneath his agitation. "Your brother is not dead."

"He will be."

She looked at him carefully. He had never shown himself to care. If anything, his lack of feeling was what had defined him before she'd enraged his human form. "And yet you say you seek no solace."

"He is just another victim of the beast."
He sneered. "One who should have known better. They all should have. Xeric, especially, deserves the pain of his arrogance. He will long live with it, as his prized mind is still perfectly intact."

There was emptiness to his words, though. An emptiness that unsettled her.

"You are still celebrated," she said. She had seen it in the mirror when she couldn't find him—their terror of him had increased, but none of the king's court had asked for punishment to be brought upon him.

"Of course I am. You can't blame the weapon for the havoc he wreaks. Even Xeric—"

"Set—"

He jerked at her use of his name. "No. We are done here, Tender. I want none of your words or your pitiful gifts. I want neither your presence nor the reminder of your existence. You will die at your time, unnoticed, as all do upon my claws. Do not come near me again."

He turned and disappeared into the trees. She watched him go, and this time, she knew he meant not to return, and a feeling of bleakness took hold of her.

Is this what it felt like to lose a friend? She hadn't had one before to gauge such a loss, but it was like a hole in her being that kept growing. The wounds from his words were nothing compared to the memory of his stark expression and the bleakness when he spoke.

How could she patch such holes?

She looked at her well of magic and knew she didn't have enough. The quarter dance that would generate the necessary abundance was still days ahead and would need to be combined with what she already could claim. Far too late to be helpful.

Though, she could—

No. Just as immediately, she pushed the half-formed thought aside.

But pushing it aside only left room in her head for the image of Set's face to revolve. For the formidable strength of his features to be covered in bleakness, then be buried in cold certainty.

She looked down at her arms—at the perfectly spaced marks of the last two hundred and ninety-four quarter dances—a testament to her service. Four more such even spaces would mark her as the best tender in history. She would be hailed as the standard for all future tenders to aspire.

All she had to do was the same thing she had done for the past two hundred and ninety-four quarter cycles. All she had to do was continue, as she had done for all the moons before, and she would shine bright in memory.

Sister? The vines said, eagerly swarming around her in their ever-hungry state, feeling her emotions before her mind grasped her own choice.

She held out her arms.

Chapter Nine: Choices

"Tender," the Southwestern Leykeeper said harshly, as he dropped his amulet on his ley point. Of all the leykeepers, the bison-wolf had always treated her with the most disdain. "What have you done? The turn was two moonrises early."

The Western Leykeeper set his amulet down as well, watching her with measured, but disappointed eyes.

She swallowed at the look in those eyes—the Western Leykeeper, an eagliger, had always been one of her largest supporters. She had been found lacking by her own tribe, and it tore at her gut.

"The Southwest Ley was given most of the influx," she said. She'd chosen very, very carefully, even in the impulsiveness of her decision. "The Beastkiller of the bison-wolves has been a proud defender of the western territories, and with the increase in attacks, I thought it prudent to aid you in whatever you have been undertaking with his training."

The bison-wolves had figured out a way to increase their favorite warrior's power and abilities through magical means, and had been using some of their allotment in the leys to do so.

Set disdained the "Beastkiller" immensely—for the immense bison-wolf always looked after himself first and foremost.

"I sent a measure of physical strengthening to all the warriors of the leys. I see that I was worried for nothing, though," she said, folding her hands together. "A mistake. I assure you that no other failures or oddities will occur."

The vines stretched around her, asking why she was saying something she didn't believe.

The Southwestern Leykeeper narrowed his eyes and looked at the vines. "I don't believe your words, Tender." He returned his gaze, darker than she had ever seen, to her. "The others were wrong about you and this action proves it. You aren't the best tender this garden has ever seen."

The Western Leykeeper stayed silent.

She swallowed against the lump swelling her throat. "You...are correct. My apologies, Leykeepers."

"Your apologies?" the bison-wolf asked harshly. "What use are your—"

"I serve the leys and the garden," she said loudly.

She had done her job for seventy-three full moons and made certain each kingdom and ley had what it needed, but she'd never spared any extra magic on his kingdom before, especially such an expenditure that would only help them in any quest for power they had. She never would have either, if she hadn't needed to cover the healing of the feldragons, who controlled the sister line as one ley struck through the Nexus and became the other.

The Southwestern Leykeeper knew he curried no favor with her, and he was incapable of bending his neck to try.

"This won't go well for you," the Western Leykeeper said softly.

And maybe it was something of Set's words that made her respond with, "Oh? What will be done?"

The Southwestern Leykeeper's eyes glinted dangerously. "You dare?"

"From where does this attitude stem?" The Western Leykeeper said, his voice suddenly suspicious. "Something has happened to cause this behavior."

He looked around the grove closely and his eyes narrowed on the connecting circle of the Northeastern Ley, and the flowers that were strewn around it.

She coaxed a few flowers to bloom sporadically around the other leys with the little magic she had left—magic that would solely work in the grove until the next Quarter Draw. "My excitement only."

She couldn't think of Set while the leykeepers watched her—couldn't think of him other than as her executioner. However, the touch of another's skin after so long without—she could think of that—and she let some of her longing spill through. "I wish for the Renewal Moon."

Something loosened in the Western Leykeepers' shoulders and his face eased. "Of course you do," he murmured. "I hadn't thought on... You will have your change, and you will be beautiful in it. But we must keep to the schedule. For the good of all."

"Yes, I know."

"I don't want you to be sanctioned," he said, voice low and comforting, rumbling with tiger purrs, even as his companion continued to vent his rage in puffs of steam. "You can still be the second best tender of the age. As long as you watch yourself these last quarter moons, you will secure your place in our histories."

"Yes. Yes, of course. I will try." The vines moved again, sensing the duality in her words.

His eagle eyes narrowed a fraction on them. "We will help you. We will be watching the Draws. We will not let you hurt your legacy further."

"Thank you," she said.

He turned with a flourish of robes and strode into the trees beyond the grove, the Southwestern Leykeeper stomping after him.

Lirah looked at her hands, glistening with green, and let a tear escape. The vines curled around her in question. Sister?

"What have you done?"

Her heart gave a lurch as Set appeared with almost no warning on the heels of the leykeepers' departure.

She swallowed. "That is the second time I've been asked that this morning," she said, trying to still her racing heart.

"Callux. Xeric. The other generals. They were broken or on death's pyre, then suddenly, the leys shake and they are without a single blemish. What did you do?"

"We have had tremors before," she said, trying to inject calm into her shaking voice.

"Not ones coinciding with an insertion into the leys. You fed the magic early. You made an error. But we both know you only make errors on purpose, Blessed Tender of the Most Sacred Grove, best of all of them."

She swallowed and lifted her chin. "Not anymore, am I?"

"What did you do?"

"The Southwestern Ley needed an influx—"

"The Southwestern Ley needed nothing but to wait three days' time. The Northeastern Ley, on the other hand, has strengthened warriors like the rest, but the same amount of magic it would otherwise, except for the surge that mysteriously occurred as a backlash from the amount you pumped into its sister ley."

"The world grows unstable. The myths rise once more. A capable mage is said to walk again in the land beneath ours—"

"No."

"The winds whisper—"

"I am far from stupid in this form. I don't care about some mage." He said the last word in extreme distaste. "I know what you did."

"You are not stupid in your other forms, either. Maybe less aware of pack dynamics—"

"Do not play games with me."

She stared at him and let the facade drop completely. "Games are not things I get to play."

She looked at the flowers freshly blooming around the ley circle. That hadn't been a game. She didn't think the leykeepers could do anything to Set directly, but they could punish the feldragons, make them suffer from magic withdrawal. It would force the feldragons into going to war against the leykeepers in order to rip the Nexus from their hands.

Many, many beings in the five kingdoms would die.

Meanwhile, the leykeepers would blight the eagligers, even the Western Leykeepeer would do it, as his duty was now to the leys, not his old tribe. They'd punish her family. Take away the tokens and reverence that had been gifted to them. Ruin them instead.

She took a painstaking moment to compose herself. "The clover near all the leys proves that every kingdom was granted a small surge." She had been very careful. "Why does it matter how it occurred? Are you not pleased your compatriots are better?"

"I care not for them." His voice was as aggressive as his movements.

"You lie," she said simply. "You do not want their deaths on your soul."

He savagely paced. "There will be other tenders," he said, as if speaking to himself.

She swallowed. "Of course there will be. I am but a single sunrise in a vast landscape," she said hollowly. A sunrise that wouldn't even be remembered now—not with the action she had taken.

He stopped pacing and his eyes narrowed. "Your edge is gone. Your calm confidence. Why did you deviate?" His tone had changed to something more suspicious than aggressive.

"I made a choice." And there was something soothing in that statement—stretching through her and taking the edge from the pain.

He looked down at the flowers around the grove, gaze focused, trying to suss out why. When he looked back up at her long minutes later, she didn't know what he had deduced, but his eyes held none of their normally vicious edge.

"If you maintain that you are but a single sunrise, you are no longer necessary. Leave your prison. You will have a head start on the trance bloom," he said quietly.

A bit of warmth filled the hollow that had reappeared in her chest in the wake of the leykeepers' visit. "You know nothing of how the garden works," she said fondly.

He showed his teeth. "I've never cared."

She wanted to ask if he cared now, but she knew the response she would receive. "The dome opens at the peak of every seventy fifth moon cycle, and only at that single peak. I accepted my fate long ago. Once inside the dome"—she held forth her hands—"there is no return."

The vines twined around her, soothing and threatening. Green chains of fate.

Ours. No sadness. One of us.

She stroked them, calming their ruffled thorns.

"You should have run when you had the chance then." Even as he said it, though, she could see the contempt in his eyes for such an act.

"To run or rebel is to betray the grove. And I am loyal to my people and the kingdoms." She tipped her head to him. "The bond and chain, and my loyalty to both, bring me comfort. Just as such things bring solace to you. And bringing you comfort, gives it to me in return. Perhaps that is my game, Dark Prince. To comfort you in my final moons."

He reached down and ripped up one of the flowers she had made to keep the leykeepers unsuspecting. "Comfort me? If you were outside your protection, vulnerable, you would fear me."

"Your savagery is in service to and in defense of your people. There is nothing to fear in that."

His mouth became slashing curves. "There is everything to fear. You healed my brethren at the cost of your legacy, but even I cannot control the trance blooms, or the

Renewal Moon's fall. Your sacrificial gesture was mistaken."

"My fate and sacrifice have long been determined. They were not the reason for my gesture." She pulled her hand along the vines and let them climb up and wind around her. "And I fear neither."

"A good soldier," he spit.

"Like you," she said. "A tender's position is not to question. It is to serve." A vine wrapped around her wrist. "And to serve is to be served."

"Taken directly from a leykeeper's mouth, I'd bet." He narrowed his eyes, and she felt their assessing weight—looking for weaknesses in her.

"It is a great honor to serve the leys."

An honor to finally prove herself as something other than the poor, disadvantaged, unchangeling who required clothing and ate a share of the kills that those who actually contributed to the village community worked hard for.

The eagliger village to which she'd been born had been exalted and protected for the seventy-three moon cycles since—the seventy-three cycles that she had existed as the Tender of the Garden.

The villagers' bright smiles and avid relief had been accompanied by the whispered promises of the leykeepers to an unchangeling child that someday transformation would be hers too. It hadn't been a hard choice to go with them.

"I chose it."

"Choice." He tilted his head back and laughed harshly. "You have eaten too many trance flowers, Tender."

She tilted her head. "I chose to accompany the leykeepers. To give myself to this. To support and protect my village. There is a choice otherwise, as you stated."

The girls that people rarely spoke about—and then only in whispers. Of the ones who had flown, tried to escape, then been hunted down. Executed as traitors. The prick of gold blood rendered a death sentence, always. The only thing to be determined was how that sentence was rendered—immediately, or after six years' of exalted service.

And the vines knew. They always knew if the chosen girl would run.

She had chosen to protect and provide for her people. To be able to call the village her people was something she hadn't even had before. And to have a chance to feel her body and spirit transform into something more...

"I can find comfort in my fate. That you will be the last thing I see, will be a magnificent sight."

"Comfort...last thing... Fear me."

She thought about the women at the revel, and the officers on the field. "I think you magnificent in all forms," she said quietly. "I would consider myself touched by the moon to spend even a single rise at your side."

"Fear me."

She looked at him, gaze seeking his—seeing the turmoil raging inside. "You do not truly wish me to fear you," she said simply.

He shouted—something incomprehensible and full of rage—and triggered a transformation right into his berserking form. He could trigger the transformation without the trance flowers, if he got emotional enough—he could just never control what happened afterward.

Nothing in the grove was exempt from his rage. Nothing exempt from his devastation...

...not even the pile of golden flowers that she had given to him—now ripped and glistening in the wreckage of the glen.

~*~

"I don't know what you want from me," he said, when he was human once more, shuddering on a growing bed of clover.

She pulled her fingers comfortingly over the moss between the leys and watched him shiver through the aftershock of the change. She sent small sprouts of fire grass beneath the clover to warm him, glad that he was in the exterior ley circle, where she could still affect him. "I don't know what I want from you either," she said softly.

Chapter Ten: Falling

He sighed as she appeared next to him at the feldragon fire revel two days later—a second celebration for his renewed brethren, who were up and walking and now making merry a safe distance from him.

"Go away," he said, lazily flicking an ember stick in the direction of the bonfire with his middle finger.

"I think I shall stay." She settled herself next to him, wrapping the watery cloak around her as she sat. She had worked herself and the garden hard, gathering all the splintering bits of magic that she could in order to be here.

It was far from the first time she'd accompanied him to a revel, but it was the first where he wasn't snapping his jaws at her.

"They all think me increasingly daft," he said. "Speaking to the air."

"They think correctly."

The response almost earned her a smile. He leaned back against the wall of vine-filled stone and closed his eyes. "Leave."

She encouraged one of the leaves of a climbing non-venomous vine to curl into his throat. "And miss the chance to watch you rave at yourself? Never."

Without opening his eyes, he pinned the leaf back in place with a retractable claw. "Speaking to oneself is considered a sign of trance fever."

The vine shook its leaf free and nestled back into the stones.

"You do look feverish," she said. His skin was highlighted by the fire with a healthy glow. She reached forward, as if to touch him, before curling the fingers of her ghostly hand into her palm. "But I think the fever agrees with you."

He opened his eyes, gaze pinning her, then leaned forward to grab his drink.

"The fever is a menace," he said, draining his tankard and throwing the empty vessel in the general direction of a servant who barely caught it—juggling six other vessels while trying to catch the seventh with his tail.

"You could have handed it to him," she said pointedly.

Set showed his teeth. "I'm neither a peasant nor a man taken to kindness. I'm a prince and an extremely terrifying one, at that."

She held his challenging stare for a long moment, then looked up at the star-filled sky, dotted haphazardly through the canopy of the mangough trees. "Your terror is only eclipsed by the beauty of the trees from which you reign. Your own view must be extraordinary—the sentinel point of the village, a wide expanse of valley and sky to view."

A group of girls came by, casting glances Set's way. His lips curved, and the slant was both mesmerizing and alarming. The girls reacted to the disparate urges caused by it in a strange way, pushing and pulling at the others in multiple directions—some wanting to approach, others outright scared.

He leaned back and looked to the sky. "I should be observing it there instead of here."

Lirah watched the girls whispering—some low, some insistently—and she scooted closer to him. The water from the garden rippled around her as she moved. She looked down at it, an idea forming, then pulled the thin sheet of it over his form.

Show me our stars, she commanded. A brilliant display of firefly light and swirling colors appeared everywhere around them.

She heard his breath catch. Who could say they'd made the beast do such a thing?

"What is this?" he demanded.

"The starlight of the dome," she said simply.

The kingdoms were full of wondrous—and deadly—things. But the firelights of magic that raced over and through the dome at night were something she'd always considered special. They were a gift of her sacrifice.

"You watch this, each night?" he asked lowly.

"Yes."

"Magic."

She nodded and set the colors swirling with a flick of her wrist. "The magic of the dome—completing the ley circuit, keeping everything in balance."

They watched the colors and lights swirl together—like the magnetic magic that sometimes drifted across the skies, but far more bright and mercurial—and the silence grew into a companionable, comforting thing.

"Why do you come here? Why do you sit with me?" he asked after the lights started dimming and the fire revel entered into its final phase of merriment—people splitting off in pairs or groups of writhing bodies.

She watched the glimmer of the water fading around them and saw her own form flicker—only enough magic left in the pond to remain by his side for a few moments more. She'd used all of what she had left in order to gift him the show, and she'd have to wait three moonrises more for the magic to renew enough for another walk.

"Perhaps it is because I like you."

The magic faded fully then, but not before she saw his expression of disbelief.

~*~

She pulled her fingers through the waters at dawn, but there wasn't even enough magic for a look in on the sapfoxling village. She couldn't even work the garden again—the magic in the kingdoms was at such a high that it would start to spill over into outside territories, if she did.

She had known what she was doing the night before, though, in spending her share—and she didn't regret it. She would be alone for a few days because of it, but she had spent many moons alone—countless ones even before her term as tender. Being alone was nothing new.

Us, us, you always have us.

She smiled down at the vines, letting them curl around her. "Of course I do. Simple greed is what has me looking for more."

Us, us. More than enough.

"You are a handful, for certain. But think of it the same way as your nature with the cluster—where you climb all over each other and me. Humans like to feel touch."

We touch.

"I know. Worry not."

"You could stop nurturing them," a now-familiar voice said, making her jerk to see Set standing outside the dome, watching her. "Stop feeding the leys."

Elation took her as she rose. She hadn't needed to use magic to see him. He had come here—to her, mere hours after she had left his side.

She steadied herself and tried to remember what he had just said. "The vines are perilous companions to those who choose not to nurture them."

"They seem to like you just fine."

"They know that I will never let them wither or die," she said, simply. The vines curled around her.

Never, never, never—not our sister.

Set's eyes narrowed on them. "But they will let you die?"

Joined, joined, die not, together forever.

"They welcome the joining," she said, petting them as they continued furiously whispering promises.

He blinked. "Joining? You will be but red scattered upon the forest floor."

"And then I shall seep into the moss and grow once more. Transform," she said wistfully, letting the closely guarded secret free in the midst of her elation at seeing him. It felt like freedom in and of itself, saying it.

His narrowed eyes took in the vines weaving around her. "Transform? Those are—"

"It is not spoken," she said quickly. For freedom or not, trouble could only result from the admission.

"Those are the previous tenders?" His face was expressionless. "You are going to die, then transform. Into a plant," he said, deadpanned.

"Well, we can't all choose forms with teeth," she said lightly. "Yet venomous barbs are not the worst weapon to wield."

"The vines..." He cocked his head, working through his thoughts. "The vines are necessary to operating the dome, the magic, and the leys. The system requires more vines. That is why you are sacrificed. They need you to die."

"Every quarter moon, one vine grows with the blood ritual," she said, gaze on the vines crawling over her feet, as the words issued from her like a river long dammed. "And every thirteen full moons, a flight is released from service. But every seventy-five moon cycles, three vines grow to lead the others." Splitting the newly sacrificed tender's consciousness between them, then splitting it again to share with the entire cluster—spreading her consciousness everywhere, and yet nowhere fully at all. "This growth is integral to the power of the garden and the kingdoms."

He contemplated her. His expression was cold, but his eyes were not. "And you want this?"

"Do I want what? To transform? To be released?" She stroked a hand along the ley nearest him.

"To be sacrificed." There was something cruel in the words and how he twisted them—an emotion behind them that spurred her own ire.

"What is the nature of sacrifice or acceptance? I have and will do the best that I can in the time allotted to me."

"Allotted," he said with a sneer.

"I find joy in the garden and the vines," she said tightly. "In doing work that benefits all."

"Joy? Is that why you follow me? For your joy? I will be your death. Do you understand that?"

"My own forfeit of life? I'm not dim, Berserker. But my death is one that will benefit everyone in the Cruel Lands. In that, my death gives joy."

"I think you claim a lack of dimness that is in opposition to what issues from your mouth."

She narrowed her eyes. "My death and transformation will allow you to keep what you have held pride in for twenty years."

"You do not know what brings me pride."

"Set Tyrne, Defeater of Olg, Blitzer of Menarc, Evil of Fel, One True Beast of Nok." She tilted her head. "Or Set Tyrne, Builder of Forgain, Dreamer of Manse, always alone?"

His expression shut completely. "Shall I return such favor? Lirah, Unchangeling of the Eagligers? Spurned by the masses for her formless shape? Companion to mere plants? Barren orchestrator of the leys?"

"I am all of those." She said it calmly, but the hint of emotion underneath brimmed with challenge. "And it gains me nothing to pretend any of them are false."

His eyes narrowed. "You think I falsely represent myself."

"You never falsely represent yourself, Berserker. You are always as you are. You just don't see it."

"I see it."

"Then you fail to understand the glory."

He leaned toward her, the dome feeling thinner in its barrier between them. "I understand all about the glory. What you are saying is that I should embrace all that I am, as if I don't understand. I embrace it every day. On the battlefield. In the boughs. I am always that which I am."

"But you think that all that you are."

He jerked back, anger fully suffusing his features. "Don't tell me what I think."

She looked down. "No. I should not." It was the one thing that had always been hers—her own thoughts. "I am sorry."

He prowled the exterior ley circle, as if her apology had only increased some internal strain. "What do you want from me, Tender?" he demanded.

She didn't respond, but her gaze stayed on him.

He observed her for long moments, pacing, then he stopped and fixed her with the intense stare that made her heart leap strangely within her chest.

"There is nothing I can do about the beast. He will kill you," he said. But this time, instead of anger, his voice held the barest hint of regret.

"I know," she said calmly. "That has never been in doubt."

"You think to make me penitent?" He asked, still trying to find her angle.

"No. Penitence doesn't suit you." She smiled.

"You wish for me to find you a way out of this?"

"No. I am simply taking advantage of what I can do. And in these last moon cycles, I'm choosing to bother you," she said lightly.

If she could have created a tailor-made companion from the beginning, she didn't think she could have been happier with anyone else. Prickly like the vines, deadly like the garden, magnificent, soul-weary, and unbroken—everything about him spoke to the girl she had been and the woman she was now.

He examined the dome with narrowed eyes, gaze going to the sheen at the top which contained the starlight and magic that she had shown him the night before. He wouldn't be able to see it now—the vines had assured her it was unobservable outside of the dome when they'd been courting her favor at the start of her term—but the memory would be enough for him to know the magic was there, even now.

His calculating gaze switched to the ley points and the flowers he had left strewn about—the flowers that still allowed him to speak to her.

He abruptly sat.

She blinked as his long legs folded into a meditative position on the grass.

"What are you doing?" she asked, mystified.

He closed his eyes, going through the ritual that allowed him to have some amount of control later if he was triggering his own transformation. "Working." He didn't allow her to respond before adding, "And bothering you while doing it."

She was unable to control her blooming smile as she let her legs fold into a mirrored position on the other side of the barrier—so close to him, she could almost pretend her hand could reach out and touch.

Chapter Eleven: Birdsong

Two days later, the sun had just hooked over the top of the sky when the beasts outside the garden took sudden flight. The excited and uncertain whispers of the vines grew as Set landed in feldragon form, great wings outspread, two linen-wrapped cages trapped in his claws. He set the cages on the ground and transformed effortlessly to human form as his feet touched the dirt.

She walked carefully to the edge of the dome, unable to contain her smile. He stared at her, frozen, seemingly unnerved by the fond expression.

He shook himself and started to remove the shroud from one of the cages.

Lirah lowered herself to a mossy seat opposite him, as she had for the past few days. "What is within?"

He looked oddly nervous as he casually finished unwrapping one. "During a routine perimeter check, I discovered them along the southern edge of the kingdom. They were stupidly chirping, bellies fat with glut. They forget their duties to the southwestern reaches. I am reminding them of their obligations."

Lirah peered between the cage's slats to see songwarblers in multiple shades of brown—their beaks moving soundlessly in aggravated motions. She remembered their song, though the memory was faded by long years without outside noise.

But the memory still brought a smile to her face. Songwarblers lifted the spirits of all creatures and beings in the five kingdoms each dawn, signifying the promise of a new day, and at each dusk, the assurance of a new night.

"What do you plan to do?" she asked curiously.

Each day the beautiful birds migrated in a clockwise fashion around the leys from the sun's rise in the east, to the sun's set in the west. At the sun's peak—now—they were usually trailing a lilting song through the south. At moon height, they would be in the north, singing all to sleep.

Set shrugged jerkily, not looking up as he opened the cages. "Encourage them." He jerked his hand, motioning for their tiny, plump bodies to exit.

The birds crept out slowly.

They were all awake, which was unusual at this time of day. They slept in shifts—carrying a companion who would sleep for most of the day, then switching positions at night—life mates caring for each other in a celebration of existence and love. They would fly awake and alongside each other, dancing in the air, in the hours between, though, and their combined song would travel through each ley they passed like the joyful midday bells of a mage's clock tower.

They lined up carefully along the edge of the southwest section of the exterior ley circle, after a long, fearful look at Set.

"Is this one of those princely things you do where you throw things at your prey to encourage them?"

Set motioned gruffly. "Very funny. Just touch that ley line."

She did so. Perhaps he thought the garden would spread their song.

The birds opened their beaks and gave their first triumphant trill.

Lirah reflexively jerked her hand from the ley and grabbed her throat. A sob caught there, strangely, and Set's eyes went wide and panicked.

She forced herself to put her fingers back upon the metal, almost afraid the sound would be gone. But the birdsong filtered into the dome again—a melody of rising triumph mixed with an undercurrent cacophony of lonely peril.

And it wasn't just auditory and visual—the thrums of their cries and song mixed with the stomps of their tiny feet along the ley, pulsing to her in a tactile rhythm. She let the beat throb beneath her shaking fingers.

"Do you not like them?" he asked hesitantly.

"I like them very well," she whispered.

They sang their song—of hope, of joy, of the journey of the sun. Her memories of their song combined with the concurrence of the moment, with the stomping beats beneath her fingers and the ringing melody in her ears—the memory enhanced by the action of the man who had done this for her.

And when it was finally over, she was too overcome to respond.

She watched Set gather the birds. Watched him aim their little bodies toward their normal flight path as they nervously chirped. A lazy swipe of his hand launched the anxious flock into the air.

They took flight along the Western Ley, back to their path. Set didn't look at her as he stuck the covering blankets inside the empty cages and closed the doors.

It struck her then, that he had collected each of them. Set Tyrne, Berserker of the Cruel Lands, had corralled each bird in order to provide her with the beauty of a forgotten song.

She reached for him, willing any magic she could to touch his cheek. To stroke it in place of the skin that she wished was sliding against his. His eyes closed briefly, and she could almost feel the press of his cheek beneath the magic.

"Thank you," she whispered.

He opened his eyes, and touched his cheek. His expression was hard to read—full of so many things. "You're welcome."

Chapter Twelve: Rippling and Turning

The Quarter Draw, with the trance blooms densely pollinating the air, brought the beast raging to the dome as the vines danced and slashed.

The next day, Set placed a mermaid's purse on the ley circle, and the sounds of the ocean roared in Lirah's ears and crashed beneath her fingers.

The following week's draw brought a darker look in his eyes and the gift of the mountains—thrilling her with the feel of ice on the ley, almost scorching her skin with cold, and accompanying the rumbling sound of snow cascading down a slope. The experience had made her smile at him for so long that he'd had no option but to return it.

More gifts had followed after that.

As often as she spent traversing the kingdoms with him now—all her free time spent at his side—it was only when he brought things to the ley circle that she could experience the smells, tastes, textures, sounds and sights of the world outside the dome that had been lost to her.

Her last full moon before the Renewal Moon rose tonight. Lirah stared at the ley that held his gift from yesterday, a golden branch from the highest mangough tree—the memories of wind, sun, and sky in its core—and a smile crept, unbroken on her face.

The vines rippled in the grove around the dome, indicating that someone was approaching, and happiness lit within her. It could not be a worshiper or leykeeper, for there were strict rules concerning the full moon dances when the garden fully renewed the leys. And it would only be two weeks' hence, during the coming new moon when a new tender was chosen, that thousands of leykeeper acolytes and Nexus worshipers would descend upon the grove en masse to witness the choosing and brave the dangers of the grove.

Creatures and beings had tried to gain a peek during a non-festival time before. Curiosity over the garden was a never-ending affair among the kingdoms. None but Set had ever survived the viewing of a dance, however, and witch tales had been passed down about what happened during a quarter moon revel.

Don't approach the grove during a quarter night, for death will greet your steps. On a full moon, even death would be desired in the descent to agonizing depths.

No, the worshipers, and even the leykeepers, made certain to maintain a healthy distance from the garden on the days of full moon rise. That meant the visitor could only be Set.

Lirah moved out of the garden's fog and toward the area where the grove was alerting her of the disturbance. The released vines were collecting again, eager for the dance they always returned for. The grove was a perilous place this close to full moon rise.

Even for Set, the full moon would be a challenge. She approached the edge of the dome, a soft rebuke on her lips.

The rebuke died.

The person at the edge of the grove wasn't Set.

A small face peered at her from the bushes and Lirah drew in a sharp breath.

The exterior vines swarmed toward the girl with cries of "delicious, tasty, fixed," and Lirah had to physically shove her hands into the ground and grab them through the garden's magic.

The vines struggled in her distant grasp, making them look like they were dancing. An expression of awe and delight mixed in the unchangeling girl's eyes, along with something Lirah couldn't parse. Fear and determination? A distant memory uneasily slid through her.

Lirah kept her grasp on the vines and shook her head sharply. Go, her actions said.

The human sapfoxling stared at the vines, then the dome, then at Lirah. Her expression turned more determined.

The girl crouched down, placed something upon the ground, then abruptly disappeared from view.

Lirah released her hold on the vines. They swayed irritably, then slithered over to swarm the token where the unchangeling had stood.

The vines curled over it and dragged it toward the dome, setting it amidst Set's gifts.

A laurel crown lay upon the ground in offering—a familiar crystal woven into the strands by a child's dedicated hands.

Lirah stared at the pile for a long time.

Chapter Thirteen: Reaching

With the full moon waning, and her access to magic back to full strength, Lirah marked the unchangeling child's latest scrape, as seen through the pool. She would give the other children something to think about—she just had to be crafty about it.

While mulling possibilities, she pulled into view the battle over the Southwestern Ley. The kingdoms' enemies were becoming craftier, utilizing the tactics of the beetlefolk, trying to gain any advantage.

It was the downside to her successful run as tender. As the magics in the lands shifted prosperously, the stability of the Nexus was increasingly coveted by those outside of it. Outside factions were banding together—uneasy allies who would turn on each other once victory was achieved.

Lirah cloaked herself in water and stepped out next to Set. His gaze was moving along the battlefield and he seemed to be brooding. Only the tightening of his fingers into fists indicated that he sensed her.

"Why have we not engaged?" Callux asked.

"The bison-wolves want their Beastkiller to have glory today," Xeric said, with a sneer, his eyes tracking the battle, but frequently returning to check the grasses around them.

If there was one thing the Crown Prince of The Cruel Lands had learned, it seemed to be that being near Set and in control of the environment was more valuable than presenting his back to the potential berserker some distance away.

"The Beastkiller has strength," Callux observed.

"But not wit. Their experiments will do them no favors when they have a raging beast on their hands that they can't control in any form—one they do not plan adequately for. When he wipes their kingdom, I will be ready."

Lirah watched the warrior in question plow through troops, an inelegant sweep to his violence. Watching Set was like watching the natural violence of nature and magic. Watching the bison-wolf warrior whose bloodlust-filled eyes never displayed anything else, was unnerving.

A troop of feldragon-allied infantry soldiers were swiped by the Beastkiller on the field and Xeric's eyes narrowed dangerously.

"We engage in five. The bisons have had their fun. Now it is time to end playtime." Xeric started striding toward the hill where the strategists held position.

"Stay here," Set said abruptly. "I will take care of this."

Both men stopped and looked at him—one in surprise and the other in narrowed contemplation. Lirah must have worn a mix of the expressions herself, as she'd watched enough battles to know that Set usually cared little for anything except when he'd be put to the field.

"When you are called," Xeric said.

"No. As soon as our allies move."

Callux looked at him in confusion. "But, that won't utilize your—"

"You will not stray from the plan," Xeric said. The eldest of the three, he showed none of the confusion of their younger sibling.

"The plan is banal," Set said dismissively. "Even you think so. You hate it. It is time to retest limits."

"Thinking isn't what you are here for," Xeric said, enunciating the words. "And limits were tested years ago. You killed three legions during the testing, though perhaps you forget."

"Perhaps. Your blood was easily wiped from my claws," Set said, with the detached coldness that he was prized for. Xeric's fingernails grew to sharpened points that clacked against the heels of his palms. "But I will test something here, all the same. You cannot stop me. For all your machinations, you never could, Xeric," Set finished.

"Test what?" Callux said, still looking confused.

"He wants to fight as a fel," Xeric said coldly. "See if he can control it, when he is barely holding the beast back n—"

"Do you want to test that?" Set asked tersely.

Xeric's lips thinned and a malevolent light entered his eyes, but he said nothing further for a moment. Lirah let her fingers pull along the scene, taking in the strung-taut muscles in Set's arms and back. Xeric wasn't wrong in his statement, and neither was Set in his threat. It would take little impetus to turn Set into his berserking form now, no less in the midst of battle.

"We need no more death, nor miraculous recoveries. You have your place, like all of us do," Xeric said tightly. "And you will fulfill it."

"Like you always do," Callux added far more eagerly—with hero worship in his eyes.

Xeric's lips tightened. "Yes. Like Set always does. Come, Callux."

Xeric strode off to where the generals were directing battle lines and the strategists from the other kingdoms were watching, Callux following in his wake.

Lirah stepped closer to Set, who side-eyed her, but said nothing.

"What are you up to?"

"If the generals had any say in the matter, nothing. Fortunately, they control less of the beast than I do. Xeric should be encouraging this. Battles that include the beast bore him."

She frowned. "What are you planning?"

"Change."

Xeric turned and gave a tight, angry nod from the strategists' circle, and an official blew the signaling horn, sending the combatants on the field scrambling. The Beastkiller hesitated, eyes cold, then leaped away, fast paws taking him into the forest.

Set rushed forward, changing midair into his feldragon form. Landing on clawed paws, he charged into the battle.

He turned berserker fifteen beats of her heart later.

She followed him through the field until the bloody end. She sank next to him, waiting for him to recover enough to speak.

"Did you discover what you wanted?" she asked.

He stared at the setting sun. "No."

~*~

He didn't seem to discover it the following day either.

During the next battle, she watched him turn in ten beats.

Then five.

The fourth battle had him turning as soon as his feldragon paws hit earth.

She lifted a brow when he was human once more. "What about now?"

"Shut up, Lirah," he growled.

The next battle he didn't bother starting as a feldragon.

"That man." He pointed to an enemy wearing a red battle pouch. "I will not kill him."

She looked at the man and shrugged. "Okay."

In the aftermath though, she saw the red pouch spilled on the field alongside the lifeblood of its owner.

During the next skirmish, Set's marker was a blue patch upon an enemy's chest. Then white war paint upon another's horns. Then the enemy whose third tail was wrung with knots.

It became increasingly obvious what Set was doing, though—especially when his eyes grew more haunted each time he failed.

But when Set's marked victim became the first to die upon his claws—the transformed beast heading straight for the marked man—the agony became too much.

Set disappeared as soon as he had enough energy to stumble to his knees and fly.

~*~

She found him, three moonrises later, on a small, flat mountaintop, lying on his back, staring into the sky.

He didn't move as her magicked moss automatically spread out and softened the ground beneath him, though he sighed.

She stretched out beside him—bare legs and feet extended—and rested her head on her arm, staring at him instead of the sky.

"You missed three battles."

"I'm sure Xeric did fine without me."

"Are you feeling better?"

"No."

She let her fingers drip magic, heating the moss beneath him. "I'm sorry."

He closed his eyes, then turned to face her. His gaze took her in and there was a small lift of his brows. "You are wearing...very little today."

She looked down her body and wondered what he saw. It was a quirk of the garden's magic—the people outside the dome saw what they wanted to see. The leykeepers saw simple ceremonial robes. The masses of worshipers saw her gowned with headdress and rich, gilt-edged fabrics.

The simple truth was that she usually walked around without much on at all. The temperature was never too hot or cold in the garden, and magic provided what she needed. There were plenty of materials in the garden for magic to fashion light clothing, and there were days she partook. But, truth be told, the vines made up the extent of her usual wear. There was a lazy ease in it, and she'd found greater power in the skin contact.

"Then you see truly."

He closed his eyes, as if some thought pained him. "The magic? I had wondered at the tales of you in robes."

"The magic shows what you wish to see."

He rubbed a hand over his face. "Great."

She laughed. "Come now, you could just believe that you wish to see the truth."

He looked over at her and didn't say anything for a long moment, then turned to look back to the sky. "I could."

She reached out a hand automatically, then curled them into her palm just as reflexively. "I'll take that as a compliment," she said, as lightly as she could. "An unchangeling with the power to tempt the dark prince."

"Imagine that," he said.

He looked down at her arms, then turned his eyes away, just as suddenly.

She frowned and looked at them. They were tinted even more now after the last full moon—a deeper undercurrent of rippling green—but he had seen their changing color before. "What ails you?"

"The moon dwindles. Don't be deliberately blind, Lirah."

"Such a countdown has always been in place," she said softly. "Think not on it. There are still two and a half quarters more that you can be annoyed with my bothering of you," she said lightly.

But this time his expression grew grimmer. "Do you really not see the problem?"

She examined his expression. "My life has had an end point for seventy-four moon cycles. It is part of the honor of being the tender."

"Honor."

"Do you fear that I will be upset that you will be my end? I am not," she said honestly. "I'm glad it is you."

"You are a particularly unhelpful friend."

She couldn't stop her smile at the designation and scooted closer. But he only looked more pained. She tapped the moss with warmth again and let the silence stretch.

"You have been targeting enemies deliberately, then trying to keep them safe," she said finally. "You think this will stop you from killing me."

"I end up killing my targets even more quickly and violently." He jerked his gaze away. "The beast has your scent. The leykeepers made certain that he did, but even more so, you have given it to him, wrapped in your flowers and gifts."

She stroked the moss, sending the comfort she couldn't bring him through touch to him by heat. "Be at peace."

"Peace?"

"It is a comfort to me, that—"

"Stop speaking, Lirah."

"I had never hoped to experience the waves and sand," she whispered, remembering the sandy beach somewhere in the Southern Reaches where she'd sat with him. Three sandy shells decorated the leys outside the dome—tokens that had given her a sense of what she would be feeling if her hand were truly touching the sand. "You are a gift—and your tokens, treasures of memory and companionship."

Somehow, despite her effort, this served only to make his expression darker.

"Treasures of memory," he spat. "You will be dead in seventeen moonrises, but I will be here."

Here alone. Again. The words drifted, unsaid, in the breeze.

She stared at him, the world shifting beneath her. "I—"

"Have you thought nothing of what I will feel when I clean your blood from my hands?" he demanded.

"No," she whispered. No, because why would she?

"It is not a comfort. It is not a gift." And suddenly, she could see all of it—all of what he was feeling—in his eyes.

A sob gathered in her throat, and she pushed back, barely holding onto the magic keeping her there.

She closed her eyes against his expression. So cruel and unexpected a result that was now so obvious.

"I...I didn't know." She had never anticipated anyone could love or miss her. It hadn't been a thought to ever cross her mind. She clenched her eyes shut against the thoughts, then forced them open to meet his gaze—not to be cowardly in her agony.

"When you first responded," she said brokenly. "It was like, like a trance flower of my own, beguiling me. I wanted—want—nothing more than to have you near. To be by your side. And the consequences of that...that you would want that too and be troubled...I never knew that could happen," she whispered. "I didn't know that it was cruel of me to seek you out."

She lost control of the magic and the pond reformed around her, pushing her to the surface. She gasped, not for breath—the magic took care of breathing in the water—but wide-mouthed, panicked inhalations of sound as she pulled herself free.

She shuddered on the grass, the vines twining around her in panic. But she didn't have enough positive emotion in her to comfort them.

The still water of the pond reflected the fading crescent moon as it made its circuit through the sky.

It wasn't until the crescent had nearly disappeared that she looked up.

Set was sitting outside of the dome, silently watching her.

"I am sorry. So sorry," she said, whispering the sentiment over and over.

He waited for her to finish, her speech trailing off in tears, before he lifted a flower from the ley—one he had previously dropped there.

He stared hard at it before carefully placing it back in its position. "I am not."

Chapter 14: Wanted

She watched Set's shaking fingers finally find their balance after his latest berserking rage against the dome—an even stronger rage than he'd ever had before. There had been no acknowledgment in his eyes this time either. There never was. It was part of what made him a killing machine without compare.

He shuddered as Lirah sent warmth through the ley nearest to him.

"I can't stop it," he said roughly.

Her hand stroked the ley, soothing him in the only way that she could. "I know."

She had thought she'd shed the emotion of guilt when she'd become tender. Sacrificing herself for her tribe had purged her need of it. But here she was again, in the sunset of her term, drowning in the emotion.

She stroked the moss, wondering whether Set could feel the strokes beneath him.

He shuddered again. "There are rumors," he said hoarsely. "As you said. Of a mage with the power to change the world, born once more."

There had been whispers—whispers on the breeze and in the eager vibrations of the garden vines.

She acted as disinterestedly as she could while looking at the banked desperation in his eyes. "There are always rumors."

He pushed himself to his knees and examined her with his slicing gaze. "You know them to be true, though."

"That there is a capable magic wielder somewhere? Perhaps." What it meant for her garden, she didn't know. If the mages decided to consolidate magic in a single layer of the world, the worlds would go to war. Such rumors were but sparks, though, far from here.

"I will find this person. Or the person who carries the leash."

"No," she replied harshly, terror curling in her.

Visitors from other layers of the world were rare. So she remembered the human mage with the gold eyes and disturbing smile who had visited the grove during a crescent moon many full cycles ago, staring inside in some internal amusement while deadly gold magic licked his skin.

Then there was the mage closer to her age, with eyes of the darkening sky, who'd stalked the dome far more recently, when Set had been angrily keeping his distance from her. The mage had been covered in two different types of magic—one, a magic that was not his, but that made the exterior vines reach for him.

He'd been a different manner of predator from the first. Powerful, deadly, but saner. Analytical, impassive death lived in his gaze, but he'd hardly looked her way before he'd made one of the exterior, ancient vines go still, grabbed it, then disappeared in the same silent way he'd arrived. The ease with which it had all happened—with no alert, no sign of a leykeeper or an activated defense measure—illustrated the power and danger that could be unleashed in angering such a person.

She had never seen anyone take a vine before. She'd rarely seen anyone survive a direct encounter with one.

"Do not seek out the mage who possesses the world-changer," she said.

He leaned forward abruptly, gaze quick and keen. "You've seen this mage?"

"I've seen two of them—the first to possess and the one swift to become."

"Describe both."

"No. I told the leykeepers when the latter stole from the grove. It will be taken care of."

She didn't want Set near that mage.

Set's eyes narrowed on the mention of theft. "What did the mage steal?"

She said nothing, but her eyes went to the vine crawling in her lap.

"He stole a vine?" Set's jaw clenched. "No one has told the kingdoms this."

"The leykeepers keep their secrets. Perhaps they have already dealt with the issue," she said.

"The leykeepers are their own puppets and no more. Describe the mage. Mages."

"No," she said, voice filled with iron. "Neither felt benign even without a world-changer at their side."

"Are you trying to protect me, Lirah of the Garden?" Set asked, laughter in his voice, but none in his eyes. They were sharp and full of feeling. "Protect Set Tyrne? He who holds the beast?"

She touched the ley nearest him and let her feelings speak for her. The laughter fell from his expression completely, leaving only something fierce behind.

"Do not doubt that I could find this mage and bring him here," he said, his voice a low growl.

"I do not doubt it. I doubt your survival in the war it would bring."

"Nothing can kill me."

"Everyone has a weakness."

He stared at her. "I have no weakness of flesh. Only a weakness of you."

She swallowed. Her throat felt strangely full again. "You cannot leave for the world of the mages."

Set's expression switched to amusement again, though his eyes were still fierce. "Can I not?"

"Your king will never allow it. And every mage would seek to capture you."

His response was a laugh. "I have no need to ask the king. And I'd like to see them attempt it."

"Mages aren't to be trifled with," she said sharply.

His eyes narrowed. "I fear no mage."

No. He'd tear a swath through their society easily enough in berserker form. But the rare mages, the few only spoken of in whispers, could deal him pain. By the hand of their masters, if not their own, for rare mages were as caged as the magical beasts their masters trapped and stole when visiting this world and lands.

"Nor the rare ones either," he said, reading her mind and responding with the certainty that only someone who never failed could accomplish.

"No."

"You cannot stop me. I'll find them. Bring them here. Have them end this ridiculous farce." He angrily gestured at the dome.

"No." She squeezed her eyes closed. "No, you can't. The kingdoms. The villages. Everything we know—"

"Everything we know? Everyone acts like any change will end our world. We are warriors. We were warriors before the Nexus, and we will be warriors after," he said savagely.

She opened her eyes, calm descending. "Yes. Yes you will be."

He gave a shout of rage. "No. That is forfeit, as you've always forfeited. I will burn the kingdom down before the Renewal Moon, if I have to."

Any descending peace fled. "You cannot. My people. Your people. The vines. All will suffer."

"How do you know?" he asked, eyes darkening. "Because the leykeepers told you?"

"Yes." It was a truth as simple as the pink trees and purple skies of the enderdawn.

"And you believe them? When they will kill you in the end?"

"The sacrifice of the tender works best with wide bloodshed and pain. The prosperity of the kingdoms depends on the Nexus," she said desperately. The vines wrapped around her, upset at the discord and the disparity of feeling.

"Seventy mage years ago, my people, your people, didn't have the Nexus."

"And then we did. A gift. And we prospered with it."

"And now we could supplant it. We could make something new."

"The prosperity of—"

"You already said that."

She closed her eyes. "And I believe it."

"Why?"

"Because believing otherwise helps me not at all," she whispered, the vines swarming around her.

"Coward."

Her eyes snapped open. "I am a flightless bird trapped in a cage. Not even a songwarbler who can fly once freed. I have only ever had the pride of my position. What song do you want me to sing?"

"A battle cry," he said harshly.

She stared at him. At the lines of war on his face. She reached out, wanting desperately to touch his cheek. The magic of the dome folded around her fingers—heeding her sudden surge in emotion—but it was an impenetrable barrier between them, as always. She stroked his cheek with magic—feeling the garden respond to her desire—touching a long-faded silver scar.

"Yes. A battle cry would be most apt," she whispered. "I can deliver a battle cry, like the front line of soldiers rushing to meet the first wave of the enemy, knowing their fate. I would rather issue a battle cry than a lament."

Frustration suffused his cheeks in angry red as he grabbed for the magic stroking down his skin. "Break this magic."

She gave one last stroke to his face—the barrier still so thin yet strong between them—then let her fingers fall. "You were made for engagement, for victory, and you will forever succeed. I was made for forfeit and sacrifice, and I will also be victorious."

"Break this magic."

"I cannot."

"Want to break it. Want something."

She had wanted something—him—and look what had resulted.

She had been a magnificent tender. She had done everything she could for the kingdoms. She had shown her worth.

He pressed against the dome, white and purple lightning shooting along his arms. "You are your worth."

She stared at where the magic was coursing into him. "You are getting hurt. Stop."

He made another sound of rage and began to pace. She sent patches of moss beneath each agitated step of his feet, wishing somewhat mournfully that she could do anything else.

When he stopped and met her gaze again, craftiness had entered his indigo eyes.

"I am Set Tyrne. I am the second son of the King of the Cruel Lands, and its dark prince. I am the beast. I am the savior of my people."

She nodded.

"I am me," he said.

"Yes," she said. "You are. And you are incredible."

On his face, lingering rage turned into triumph. Disquiet ran through her, and a vine curled around her ankle in response.

He sat on a large swath of her moss and set his hand down on the ley at his left. "You are Lirah of the Eagligers," he said, almost gently. "Unchangeling. Tender of the Garden. Guardian of the Five Kingdoms. And you are wanted."

She put a hand to her mouth, but couldn't hold back the sounds from her throat and the tears coursing down her cheeks.

Chapter 15: Lamentation

The leykeepers approached the dome. "The choosing is upon us, Tender. The Hunger Moon is finished, and the half cycle before the Renewal Moon rises as the darkness without moonshine." He drew a dark circle in the grass with a hoof, then wiped it clean. "Every girl of age is assembled, and a new tender will be chosen as darkness rises."

She dipped her head. "May gold guide her steps."

The Western Leykeeper bowed, his kind eyes shining. "It has been an honor to serve with you, Tender."

She nodded back to him. "And you, Leykeeper."

The others paid their respects, some with the kindness of the Western Leykeeper, others with the more reserved graces of their people. The Southwestern Leykeeper examined her with suspicion but bowed and moved on.

But unbeknownst to them, because of Set's gifts, she could hear them in the exterior circle without their amulets placed on the points—hear them even though their mouths were pointed in the opposite direction purposely so that she couldn't read their lips.

"Who do you think it will be?" the Northern Leykeeper asked him as they walked through the grove.

"Each of the girls is malleable, as a tender should be," the bison-wolf said dismissively. "It matters not to me which of them is chosen, only that she be obedient."

Emotion coiled in Lirah. Anger. She was surprised at the emotion for a moment, then angrier still. Only long practice kept any expression from her face as the last leykeepers finished bowing to her.

She had wondered at her replacement—at who the new tender would be. She had followed the rumors through the pond, and with every gift that Set left, her ability to hear extended farther in the forest around the grove. Most were betting on a girl from the mantisbear tribe who had an extraordinary way with plants. The released vines treated the girl well enough when she came upon them.

Others said it would be a girl born from the squirrelfoxes, known for her kindness and beauty.

The excitement of the vines thrummed around her as she stood at the edge of the dome, watching people from every kingdom gather to watch the ceremony begin.

A massive crowd took up every spot in the grove and beyond, as the blood sun set behind the treetops and darkness began its descent.

Choosing a new sister, a new sister comes!

"The sapfoxlings have an unchangeling," a man was saying near the front of the northern section of the crowd, the words heavy on his seal lips. "Ten pieces on that girl."

Lirah froze.

"Not a chance," another said.

"Happened before, didn't it?" the first argued. He motioned at Lirah. "The current tender is an unchangeling. Would have won a mint by betting on her last time. I don't care what you say. Ten down."

Lirah held a hand to her stomach, as an ache began to spread inside.

She had been the first unchangeling to become tender. Why would she have thought she'd be the only?

"It will be the mantisbear," the first said.

Lirah quickly wiped her expression clear. Of course it would be the mantisbear.

Just like it had been the vampstag, the betting favorite during her own choosing.

She swallowed. The mantisbear girl. Of course it would be.

The girls continued trekking onto the ceremonial grounds but the vines only began swaying when the sapfoxling entered.

No.

"Tender," the Western Leykeeper said, motioning quickly over his dropped amulet.

It took a moment for Lirah to make her arms extend. The worshipers and revelers wouldn't be able to see the vines sink their fangs into her through the light fog meant to conceal it—they wouldn't know that she was the only thing controlling the exterior vines from consuming all of them.

The released vines had been there for Lirah's choosing as well—a silent threat in their swaying bodies.

The vines began their strikes and she absorbed the pain of the poison with long practice. Her gaze was pinpointed on the ceremony playing out in front of her, not on the frenzied dance that whirled around her, green and purple flitting through the white fog like a roiling mass of dual-colored snakes.

At least fifty girls surrounded the fire now, in an order chosen by the leykeepers. The first held out her arm and the Eastern Leykeeper pricked her wrist. Red.

Red, red, black, brown, red—the pricks continued quickly until the predesignated point of the circle was reached. Then the body language of the leykeepers shifted forward, looking for that drop of gold.

The mantisbear girl extended her arm, and Lirah held her breath. A drop of red dripped down her skin.

Lirah swallowed. She tried to concentrate on the pain in her arms instead, but nothing was working.

Brown, red, black, red.

A familiar face peered at her from the lineup as the girl drew closer to the choosing, and the vines grew increasingly frenzied.

Dozens of potentials remained behind her as the unchangeling extended her arm, but certain dread had already seeped into Lirah as the vines began moving faster.

Sister, sister, new sister.

No. Lirah swallowed. No.

The leykeeper pricked the girl's skin.

Not gold, not gold...

Slowly, a single drop fell, shining in the moonlight.

It splashed its seal of death upon the ground and the vines swarmed.

~*~

The ceremony had continued long into the morning—the revelers obscene in their merriment. It had only been diligent practice in repressing all emotion that had kept her from losing her grip on the exterior vines and letting them consume every last reveler.

"Wouldn't that have been an ideal way to end my rein?" she asked Set when he appeared. "They could have given me the title Terror of the Nexus."

Set narrowed his eyes, taking in her face, her shaking hands, and the vines swinging wildly around her. "What is wrong?"

"The Choosing." She shook her head, unable to choke out anything more.

"You knew it would occur." He looked around the grove, as if seeking out an enemy, but the leykeepers had ushered everyone out hours ago, and only the physical reminders of the celebration remained. "Not that I don't approve of your desire to do some ill, but the event itself was not a surprise."

"The child..."

A look of discernment replaced his seeking expression. "She's an unchangeling. You know her?"

"No, I know her not." Other than the day the girl had brought her gift, peeking through the bushes at the edge of the grove, Lirah had never seen her outside the mirror of the pond.

"But you have fondness for this child."

She shook her head. "No."

"Liar," he said, almost blandly.

She met his too-knowing eyes, then closed her own. "Yes. Lies are all that I have left."

"Lirah, look at me."

She did, only to find him examining her far too closely.

"You sought her out of recognition? You watched her. Like you watched me." His grasp of the matter was far outstripping any information she had given him, but he knew her—it hit her like a stampeding horde—he knew her. No one...no one had ever cared to know Lirah. "You comforted her."

"I infected her," she whispered. "The gold...I did it. The vines want her, recognize her. I infected her." She looked at him and clutched a leaf winding around her throat. "I've infected you."

"As if a beast could be infected. Should you not be celebrating this instead?" He smiled unpleasantly, but his eyes were intent. "This child you love will be one with you, too, in but a little over seventy-five moon cycles of service."

She shook her head. "I—"

"You do not feel such a way, then, when it is not you? You understand what another might feel about such sacrificial tripe?"

The look on his face was of unceasing torment. Of agony over what a short time was to bring.

"I am sorry," she whispered.

It seemed such a cruel twist of fate to give her this here at the end of her life. Or maybe it was a gift—this taste of normality and spark of promise—even though it could never be acted upon.

"Then do something. Want something," he demanded.

"It doesn't matter what I want," she said, nearly on a sob.

"It always matters." He pressed a suddenly clawed hand against the dome and the painful shocks made his human muscles tense, but he did not move his hand. "What do you want, Lirah, Tender of the Garden?"

She opened her mouth, but nothing emerged.

"What do you want?"

"I... I don't want the child to be Tender," she confessed in a rush of denied feeling.

The vines curled around her. Why, why, why, why...? they asked, restless and upset.

"Not because of you," she tried to assure them. "For her, for her—"

"I asked what you want," Set said harshly.

"I want everyone to be—"

Set banged against the magic of the dome, ignoring the blinding pain that he must be feeling. "What do you want?"

"I want to feel," she cried. "I want to transform, I want to run with you."

The vines twined around her legs, their venomous tips stroking her skin in confusion and alarm.

The savage expression on his face was pleased. "Then I will find a way."

Chapter 16: Resistance

S et

The vine wove a serpentine path along the floor as Set waited for the council meeting to end. He only attended those that he felt were most important—anger at irritating council members had triggered him to shift once, and though Xeric always had plans half-formed should Set turn to the beast, no one had escaped that episode unscathed.

He was allowed to do as he desired—attending a nitpicking review on a border skirmish hadn't remotely been on his agenda. But he had tales to spin to his father and very limited time to put forward his plans, so he waited alone.

The vine weaved closer. It must have laboriously worked its way up the mangough tree—a feat, as the king's castle was held in the boughs of the largest tree in the forest.

At one time he would have been shocked that it had found him in the king's castle, and not in his own manse, but seeing one never prompted surprise anymore. They kept coming, finding him everywhere. And even though he had beheaded the first one, and the second, they kept coming—regenerating—lacking anything close to fear.

He looked at the greenery twining around his ankle. "Tenacious like your mistress, aren't you? No fear within you."

No fear within her, except when it came to his safety and well-being, or that of another unchangeling waif. He closed his eyes at the feelings invoked by the thoughts. He wished she had more fear for her own welfare.

The vine slid up his ankle, weaving back and forth as it ascended. He bent and lifted the little plant and let it wrap around his wrist. There was a comforting weight to the vine—to the way the leaves settled, stroking along his skin.

The venomous tips lightly caressed his flesh—a comfort and a subtle warning of danger.

His brethren would pull forth scales immediately to arm themselves against a venom-filled strike, but the duality in the comfort and danger against his bare skin brought only pleasure to Set.

He looked at the vine curling around his wrist. It was unafraid of him, though in the beginning he had certainly killed his fair share of them, temporary death or not.

Unafraid of him, like their mistress.

A leaf brushed his skin, as if knowing that he was thinking of her.

"Why would you allow her death?" he asked.

It pulsed with a feeling of not death, not death, rebirth, sister, together. As a result of his extended communication with Lirah he was able to understand them to a small extent. The vines that were freed of the dome had more agency than the hive mind that existed within, but they all seemed to desire the same thing.

"You just want to be with her as well," he said, letting the venomous red tip gently slice the skin of his thumb. He examined the thin cut, and the boiling beneath. "That I understand this does not mean I will not fight that choice."

Hers, hers, hers, loves us, will not hurt us, wants to be with us.

"But you know there is more that she wants."

Sister, together, safety, throng.

And this was the opening he had been waiting for. "You have that now, do you not? She is your sister now, even though you are outside and she is within. Can you see no other way?"

The vine paused, then tightened. Lamentation replaced certainty. No other way. Death of garden. Death of lands. The magic dictates terms.

"I will fight you. All of you."

We know.

The vine sliced his skin again in warning and regret.

The door opened. "Bunch of blithering—" In human form, Xeric stopped in his tracks. His gaze focused on the vine that continued to whisper against Set's skin, all anger disappearing behind a blanching facade as his feldragon form slowly formed along the tendons of his legs and the skin of his fingers—ready to burst forth completely at the least sign of need.

"Change into the beast, brother," Xeric said, gaze never leaving the vine wrapped around Set's arm. "And I will barricade the door behind me."

"You desire a change in the décor of this hall?" Set asked blandly. "I didn't realize you hated it." He let his thumb pull over the stem resting on his skin.

"You are holding a Caliverias Vine," Xeric said slowly, as if this was an unrealized detail.

"I'm aware," Set said, letting it curl around his wrist.

"An old one."

The ancient ones were famed for being less stable and more given to their own machinations the longer they were free of the garden and Nexus. Now that Set knew that the split consciousness of all the tenders before was shared amongst them, it wasn't nearly so surprising that they were given to fits of instability. Having so little sanity spread amongst so much power...

Sister, together, throng, always, never alone.

"What is this?" Xeric murmured, as if he had heard a whisper of it.

Set tilted his head at the vine. "But you are free from the rest," he said to it.

Always one.

"With what have you been playing, Brother?" Xeric's words, though still low, were becoming increasingly demanding.

Set focused on Xeric and raised a brow. "Can a beast not have a pet?"

"Not when that beast is you."

Set smiled, showing his teeth. "True."

Xeric said nothing for a moment, but when he spoke, dawning realization and horror colored his voice. "Callux was not to survive, yet he made a full recovery from the beast's attack. Better than full."

Set didn't respond for a moment. He extended a claw from his fingertip and ran it down the vine. It shivered and curled more tightly, seeking the threat instead of shrinking from it. "And you? You walk without aid."

Xeric watched, lips tight. "You disappeared for days. You took your histrionics to the witch?"

Set's eye twitched at his brother's reference to Lirah, and Xeric's body stiffened automatically in defense. The vine tightened its grip, and Set forced himself to relax.

"Is that what plagued me?" he asked musingly, looking at the open window the vine had entered through. "Histrionics?"

"Your trials seeking control, Callux's recovery, the early quarterly magic..." His gaze shot to Set's as he pointed at the vine. "One of her vines hangs upon your wrist. You were responsible for the early quarter renewal. What deal did you strike?"

"No deal. More's the pity." For Lirah would adhere to deals made.

Xeric narrowed his eyes. "You've doomed us, in some way. There is no other explanation for that accursed plant around your wrist. What have you done?"

"Not enough," Set said coldly, answering a far different question than the one asked. "But that is going to change. For too long I have allowed apathy to drive inaction."

"You've never cared."

"You never noticed whether I cared."

Xeric shifted his body, his intelligent gaze moving with lightning speed—new plans forming within plans he no doubt already had. "Your change in behavior will be noted with the king and council."

Set peeled his lips into another edged smile. "I can't wait."

Xeric, not a coward, still extended his claws further in response to that smile. "The Southwestern Leykeeper's insinuations are true. His arguments will gain traction. His talk of repercussions—"

"Kowtowing to those amulet-wearers gains us nothing."

Xeric looked at him as if he'd suddenly transformed into a dancing ladybug. "It gains us magic. Painless transformation. You would be nothing without your berserking ability." Xeric's tone turned bitter. He had never made it a secret that he wished for the skill.

"I best you in combat without it," Set said.

"Because no one fights you in earnest, lest any of us trigger the beast."

Set examined Xeric's defensive posture. "Then that makes you weaklings. And stupid.
The beast only appears when specific circumstances dictate."

Xeric's lips thinned. "I am neither weak nor stupid."

"Then you would realize the leykeepers who harvest the trance flowers have too much power."

"They make you strong."

"I am already strong."

"You are nothing without your ability."

Set examined him. "I would have agreed with you, moons ago."

"And, what? Some unchangeling girl changed your mind?"

"No." He looked at the deadly vine softly curling around his forearm. "I changed my mind."

"You have embraced madness."

"Relying on weakness and tradition will be our downfall."

"You dare. Our traditions?"

"You say it as if a tradition should be maintained just because it is defined by the word. Weakness. That is what relying on tradition for its own sake is."

"Like the position of tender?" Xeric's tone turned challenging as his eyes narrowed on the vine.

"This all stems from a weakness you have for the priestess of the leys and garden. I can see it when you look at that vile thing about your wrist. An unchangeling girl thrice enchanted and damned? One you will kill? You are a fool."

Set bared his teeth. "And you, more so."

Xeric bared his own in return, but his eyes were swimming with narrowed new plans—a reflection of whatever was happening in his diabolical mind. "You will be arrested."

"I do not care what you do."

Xeric's gaze turned darker. "You never have."

Set started laughing. He laughed so hard that it took the vine winding around his shoulders to get him to stop.

Chapter 17: Consequence

The consequences of baiting Xeric were swift.

Spies had been listening to every word. Of course they had. Set lived his life without care to guard his tongue. Who was going to punish him? Xeric's strategic mind, though, always accounted for someone else listening in. It made Set wonder.

And so here he was, in the discussion chambers that he had been avoiding, waiting to see what action to take when they tried to decide his fate. If Set were anyone else, he'd be imprisoned in the stone quarry already. But even in a gathering of powerful decision makers, everyone but Xeric and Callux maintained physical distance from him.

He amused himself by watching the leykeepers uneasily cast glances at the vines peeking through the window panes.

"What has occurred?"

He didn't twitch to see Lirah settling next to him, no doubt alerted by her pets that something was happening.

"A simple matter of taming the beast," he said, in a voice low enough to go unnoticed.

Lirah watched the proceedings—a frown pulling her brow into worried lines. She was lightly clothed in creams and tans, but her arms were bare, and the magic, like always, made her hair lift and flow in mesmerizing ways, as if she was made of the vines themselves. It was hard to keep his gaze focused elsewhere.

"Are they punishing you?" she asked softly. "For my folly?"

He examined her, and saw the guilt and despair, but also the firm spine she had been developing. She didn't regret all of her "folly."

"There is little they can do to me," he murmured. "I'd like to see a leykeeper try."

The Southwestern Leykeeper's narrowed gaze was the one that kept returning his way. Bison-wolves thought themselves equal to the feldragons because they also controlled multiple segments of the leys. Their land had been equally as vicious as the Cruel Lands had once been. But now fertile and full, the bison-wolves, unlike the more battle-focused feldragons, were becoming soft.

The leykeepers, like Xeric, had easily pieced together the puzzle once they had a part of it. Lirah's early-quarter actions, the wayward day of the songwarblers, Set's behavior and increasing disobedience—all of it combined to put forth a definitive picture.

"You are forbidden from going to the Nexus," the king commanded.

Set smiled.

The Southwestern Leykeeper's eyes narrowed further, and he removed something from the pouch at his waist. "I have a better plan."

Between one blink and the next, Set felt his head hit the table, Lirah screamed, and all went dark.

~*~

"Where is he?" Lirah asked, standing at the edge of the dome as the four leykeepers with the main directional leys—north, south, east, and west—chanted. She could feel her access to the magic of the garden diminish with each intoned word. "What have you done to Set?"

The Southwestern Leykeeper growled at her. "Nothing that concerns you. But I will make certain all know how cowardly you viewed your end."

"I'm not a coward," she said quietly.

"You would subvert the Nexus. Doom us all. Just so you can live."

The words twisted within her. "I have done everything asked of me."

"You haven't done enough," he said, spittle flying from his changing lips as he lost control of his transformation. "You haven't died."

"Leykeeper," another voice said harshly. Lirah looked over to see the Northeastern Leykeeper frowning. "Get control of yourself."

"She is plotting against us," the bison-wolf shouted.

"We have taken care of it," the Northeastern Leykeeper said, continuing to frown. "But no good comes from such harshness of deed or word."

"She has always been a problem," the Southwestern Leykeeper seethed. "You've just never bothered to notice. And the next tender will be just as bad. We will be ruined unless we take further measures."

Lirah looked at him with new eyes. "You hate unchangelings."

"You are unnatural," he spit.

"Leykeeper!" the Northeastern Leykeeper said with outrage. "Should you continue such language, I will recommend your removal. We protect the inhabitants of all of the kingdoms, including those without ability to transform."

"What have you done with Set?" Lirah asked, voice growing harder, gaze focused on the being who hated her.

The bison-wolf pulled himself together. "You are worried for the beast. You should be worried for yourself."

"Why? Has my fate changed?" she asked, extending her arms. "I'm no coward. What did you do to him?"

"The Terror of the Kingdoms? He is asleep. Dormant. He will be called upon when needed, and remain docile in stasis when not."

Horror hit her equal to when his head had hit the table. The feldragon king and youngest prince had been outraged, but the leykeepers had pacified them with quick words and promises. Only Set's older brother had kept his narrowed eyes on his brother's fallen form.

"You are going to use him like a beast—you aren't even going to pretend he is anything else—and you will keep him locked away in his own mind when he is not in use."

"He has always only been a tool."

"The King of the Cruel Lands will not stand for it."

"He knows his duty to his people. And if he doesn't, his reign will be much shorter."

She looked sharply at the Northeastern Leykeeper. "You are of the Northeast—you hold one of the Cruel Lands' leys. You will defy your king? Do you think this just?"

The Northeastern Leykeeper looked at her in pity—the type of look that she was far too used to receiving from eight men who thought they knew best. "We do what we must to secure all the kingdoms, Tender. It is our duty, just as fighting is the Dark Prince's, and sacrifice is yours."

"I do my duty for the good of the kingdoms and all who live within."

"As will be witnessed."

"No." She lifted her chin. "I've done my duty every single quarter of seventy-four cycles of the moon. Two hundred and ninety eight completed renewals. That you cannot figure out how to renew the magic of the Nexus without killing the tender is a deficit of yours, not mine."

The Northeastern Leykeeper jerked back. The Southwestern simply shook his head. "I told you. Increase the ritual further, I say."

She looked at the trails of magic they were extending. "Your new ritual takes a lot of work. I know how you like your fanapple blossoms and fertilized moondrop wine—sometimes four or five times a night, Keeper of the Southwest."

The Southwestern Leykeeper smiled tightly. "I will happily complete each cycle until the Renewal Moon and drink an extra draught to your end on that night. My brethren will complete the task the feldragons cannot."

"A new executioner?" At least this would spare Set having her blood upon his claws. "Who?"

He smiled. "The task will be undertaken by the one who will rise to take Set Tyrne's place in the hierarchy of the kingdoms. You'll never see your beast again. And soon, we will have his power."

She watched the Beastkiller emerge from the timberline, his soulless eyes fixed upon her.

~*~

Set woke suddenly and completely—and the only thing that stopped a full change into his uncontrollable form was the last scream from his memory. He needed to be aware, to point the beast, just a moment longer.

"You weren't wrong."

Set jerked his gaze to the person at the top of the stone quarry who was looking down. "Xeric."

"How low you've fallen," he said cheerfully, swinging one leg.

Set looked around the stone cell. Fresh sprigs of rootwart and reviver littered the floor. He lifted one, knowing Xeric had been the one to drop them. "A quarry cell? Even unconscious for a few moments, do they really think—"

"A few moments? No. You weren't supposed to wake until the next engagement. The leykeepers were quite adamant about that."

"How long have I been out then?" Set asked tightly, taking stock of his hunger and the general feel of his body—like he did every time he emerged from the blackness of the beast's transformation.

"Three moonrises. Not yet long enough for your human to die."

Set closed his eyes and nodded. "Are you here to try and kill me, then?"

Xeric tilted his head. "I would have tried that without waking you. I know three ways that have a chance of success, long tucked away in my mind."

"Only three? I'm surprised."

Xeric's lips lifted the barest amount at the edges of his mouth. "Perhaps it is more."

Set looked around his stone prison and stretched to regain the feeling he would need. He could see the small mage device clasped loosely in Xeric's fingers that...discouraged...eavesdropping. "What is your play?"

"They think me overjoyed at your predicament—and as it is truth, it is an easy one to display. The leykeepers foolishly guard less in my presence and in their haste to keep you unconscious. I saw their trance flower stores. They intend to keep you a mindless beast, and when their plans become apparent to the kingdoms, they will likely prevail against father's outrage due to their grip on the magic that holds us all hostage."

"You want to war with the leykeepers?"

"To secure the magic directly for ourselves?" He twirled the device. "Perhaps. It is a tempting thought."

"You could keep me in here, a slave to the magic and beast."

"I could. But though I loathe you half of every day, you are my brother, and you are useful to the kingdom in other forms."

Set met his eyes. He understood what Xeric was saying. "I feel the same."

The lift of Xeric's mouth grew. "They have assigned a new executioner."

"The Beastkiller, no doubt. They should plan for two deaths, then," Set said, stretching the last of the tightness from his muscles.

Xeric gave a low laugh. "Yes." He dropped a pouch down the hole. "For the kingdom. For feldragon glory."

"Thank you."

Xeric tapped a finger against his device. "I do not know if you will save her or slay her. I believe it will be the latter, and I am not certain the former won't end us all. But it needs to be a feldragon that holds the position of executioner. We gain magic from it—though the leykeepers try to keep it a secret. Everyone except the Beastkiller and the leykeepers have been magic-banned from the grove until the Thirteenth Tender arises. They hold a constant ritual around the dome. I cannot penetrate that magic. But you have done it before, haven't you?"

Set nodded.

Xeric's lips twisted, jealousy riding the last of its waves. "Of course you have." He rose. "The bison-wolves have been encroaching on butterfly territory for many moons, and with the extra magic, they might make a true move. Even though we are clearly the betters of all, if the bison-wolves gain three segments of the leys, it will equal our territory, and they will rule more land than I am comfortable with."

"How did they get me here?"

"They have developed a hybrid trance flower that keeps the beast knocked out. I should have thought of it long ago." He examined his claws.

"It would only work for, at most, a week of doses. Now that I know it exists, perhaps less time than that. It's a stupid plan."

Xeric looked up, already smiling. "Oh, I know. I should have said that I did think of it long ago, and dismissed it for far better plans. The leykeepers aren't the strategists they think they are." He dragged his thumb down the tips of his claws. "I'd wipe the board with them if I decided to do so."

Set smiled viciously and lifted the magic-sealed pouch of flowers Xeric had collected, along with the slip of paper, attached by a piece of thread to its throat. It held a name. A mage's name. "Your boredom made you jealous. You have been too long without a challenge."

"I'm hardly jealous of a beast," Xeric said.

"Sitting on the sidelines, fighting the same boring battles—tedious. You only think the berserker state is exciting because it offers change."

"Perhaps," Xeric said after a long moment. He tilted his head. "Perhaps that is the truth I will find like you have found yours."

"The world might be completely changed, come the new moon."

Xeric looked down on him, silhouetted by the fading sun. "That does sound exciting."

"You wish to overtake me still," Set said with humor.

"Of course."

"Good. I look forward to it."

A demonic grin appeared above him. "Moonspeed, Brother." Xeric disappeared.

Set gripped the pouch of sealed flowers and the identified name, and prepared for destiny.

Chapter Eighteen: Choosing

The dome stretched over her, crackling and swirling with ghostly white light. It was her sanctuary and prison; her commitment and sacrifice.

She closed her eyes.

Lush vines twined lovingly around her as the leykeepers held their positions around the ley points of the exterior ley circle. The dark energy and magical promise of divine ability brimmed beneath their skin as they used their eight points to channel the magic of the garden into themselves and away from her.

They weren't taking any chances—the chance that she could contact Set, which they had pieced together, the chance that she could influence the next tender, who had looked quietly pleased the day after the choosing, when Lirah had checked in on her using the mirror of the pond. Or the chance that she could somehow magic a way out of the space that had held her for so long.

The vines coiled. Sad. Your magic, not theirs. We will punish them for this, when you are with us.

"It's okay," she soothed.

Yes. Soon. Together!

She smiled for them, dredging up her best one. "Yes."

Sad about the joining, too, why sad?

"It's nothing."

Something. Not nothing.

"I...loved him."

Love us. Love us!

"Of course." She stroked their leaves, glistening in the falling sun. "A different kind of love, I think. But a yearning, all the same."

He tried to take you. Death of garden. Death of lands. Even now, he tries to court our death with instruments of Blue.

She looked at them, mystified. She had never heard of anyone or anything referred to that way. "Blue?"

Death. Root-maker's guide.

Unease slithered through her. Blue eyes and magic. Would it be better to think Set unconscious in a cell, but still alive, or out making deals with the world-changer's leash holder?

"I won't let you die," she assured them. "Where is Set?"

Sad. You said you wanted to run with him, they said, ignoring her question.

"Yes," she answered wistfully.

Yet your feet move slowly.

She smiled. "It's more the sentiment of it." She reached toward the low sky of the dome and let her fingers softly dance in the air. "To feel the skin of another like you do in your clutch."

You said you wanted to transform.

"And I will." She smiled. "With you. All will be well."

But they slithered in agitation. All was well before he came.

"And all is well now. A different well. Where is Set?"

Running. Sadness. Ours. Yours. Ours.

A shock of magic vibrated through her in warning. "Stop speaking, Tender," the Northern Leykeeper said. "We cannot hear what you whisper, but know that we are listening."

Lirah rubbed her arms. The leykeepers were revealing all sorts of new powers. The vines swarmed against the interior of the dome, threats issuing from the scrapes of their leaves against the ground.

"What are they doing? Make them stop," the Southern Leykeeper demanded, looking spooked as older vines crept in along the edges of the grove.

She looked at the leykeepers. "Or what?"

In the past she had held back the question, but this time she voiced it fully.

"Your family will suffer for anything that happens between now and the Renewal Moon," the Southwestern Leykeeper said, with an unpleasant smile.

She called the vines back and let the smug expression form on his face before saying, "Should you touch one of them, know that every gaffer and ancient vine will not rest until each of you is dead."

His expression was wiped away, and Lirah allowed the vines to gather in her lap as she switched and held the gazes of each leykeeper in her view.

They thought her a meek girl. They had put a meek girl into this garden. She got to decide whether she stayed meek.

And she had decided not to be.

The garden shivered beneath her. She put her hand on the moss, feeling the magic swirling, even though she was unable to influence it now. The natural magic of the garden had been superseded by the leykeepers' attempts at control.

"Do you think this ritual that you have been holding for three moonrises—and plan to hold for ten more—will be without repercussion?" she asked. "You court outside attention with such things."

"It will be on your head," the Western Leykeeper said sadly. "Should something ill befall the Nexus or kingdoms."

"No." She smiled. "No, it will be on ours."

The shiver, turned into a tremble, and the tremble into a shake.

"Call the Beastkiller," a leykeeper said sharply.

"It isn't time," another argued.

"Something isn't right. He must be on hand, just in case."

The Southwestern Leykeeper signaled to a butterfly, and it flew off, off to find the bison-wolf who would be her new executioner.

The Beastkiller appeared a scant slip of the sun later. His eyes examined her with little emotion.

She was a stranger to him and he would enjoy killing her.

"If the magic falls, kill her," the leykeeper said.

"It will be done."

"Enter." The Southwestern Leykeeper lifted the edge of the magic that was keeping everyone else sealed outside the external ley circle. The Beastkiller strode toward it.

He never made it.

Set burst into the clearing in feldragon form and Lirah's jaw dropped as he sunk his claws into the stomach of the bison-wolf's most renowned fighter, then flung his body to the side.

It wasn't even a fight. It never was with a berserker, and people seemed to forget that Set was part of all his forms.

Set dove inside the opening before the Southwestern Leykeeper could seal it.

"A death sentence! You will die!" The Southwestern Leykeeper yelled, thrusting his hand into his pocket.

"Pull out your trance flowers and try," Set said, human once more and prowling the edges around the exterior ley circle. He held up a pouch.

The skin of the butterflyman of the South blanched of its usually sweeping colors. "You will kill us all—everyone in the kingdoms?"

"Perhaps."

Lirah looked at the pouch in confusion. But before she could ask what was in it, the world started to shake around them.

"What is this?" the butterfly asked in panic.

"The world-changer," Lirah murmured, as the magic that was going to the leykeepers stuttered, and a bit of it swam under her skin. Somewhere, in a far distant land, the world-changer was pulling magic to him.

No, something about that thought felt slightly off as the magic connecting the Nexus' dome to similar magic so far away washed through Lirah again. The world-changer was pulling magic to her. The world-changer was a girl.

"Grab the magic," the leykeepers were shouting frantically. "Harness it. We can use it."

But like a bolt of lightning hitting a metal rod, the connection that the leykeepers had created to keep Lirah contained was the tallest point that the world-changing event elsewhere was connecting to.

Every leykeeper was flung backward, and trance flowers burst in a slow motioned rupture from each one's pockets—like spice tossed in water. The dome started to shatter.

Ironic, she thought, as the shards of magic fell, that of all things, a faraway event and the leykeepers' themselves were going to induce the dome's early collapse and trigger Set to berserk, as the final ceremony would not. She was still going to meet her demise at the end of his claws.

It didn't matter, in the end, what gender or form the world-changer took, or what was happening elsewhere. What mattered was the way this would end.

She looked at Set, crouched near the leypoint where he had laid each tribute, a futile gaze staring up at her through falling glass. He'd been the only one in the exterior circle not touching a ley when the magic had hit, and therefore, was the only one still conscious.

"It's not supposed to happen like this," he said frantically as the dome shattered in a slow fall of rain.

It was as if the world was giving her one last goodbye.

"You sought the mage I told you to avoid," she said, calm enveloping her.

"Three days' hence, he was to—" He shook his head. "Something happened at the mage event. The warriors all fled. And so too then did I."

"Idiot. You put yourself in the midst of the annual mage competition?"

"Competition. I could have gutted half of them before the first spell was thrown," he said coldly. "This one, though... Perhaps. He said that if the world-changer couldn't come in three days, that he would fight the beast on the Renewal Moon. He seemed pleased at the thought. But he is gone. Something has happened in his mage kingdom."

She looked up. "The world-changer is angry and grief-stricken," she said dimly. She could hear the vines, elated and arguing. "She will rip the worlds apart."

The change started ticking over him, as her time for goodbye ran dry.

"I don't have enough control for this," he said, the change ticking over him. "I had some for... I thought I could..."

"I am happy for this," she said softly, as the glass delayed its fall one single moment more, and his face filled her view. "For you to be the last thing I see."

The air crackled, and everything shattered. Wind propelled the air, plants, and magic into high speed, whipping like a cave storm. Magic flew in all directions—eddying around the garden like a life-giving element. Trance flowers swirled everywhere, and the features on Set's face lengthened into something fiercer and more feral.

And the only thing that would be in his path was her.

"Run," he said.

But there was nowhere to run. The vines were securing her now, swarming around her in slithering waves that she had seen in their memories—this was how the death of a tender began.

But the vines were bursting with more magic, power, and purpose than even memory had shown.

Magic was shooting up and curving down into the earth, into another layer, in an event likely approaching apocalyptic. And the leykeepers, in their ignorance and fear, had made certain through their ritual that if something were to gather a magic the type of which existed in the dome, that it would call here.

"I cannot," she said, acceptance for herself, but grief for him in her voice.

"No," he said harshly, trying to back away as his transformation slowly chipped pieces away and reformed them into something even stronger. Magic was arcing over him, diving into the ground behind. She saw him contemplate it, contemplate stepping into the path.

She outstretched a hand. "No. No, please."

"You would have me be your death instead?"

"Not death."

"It is death."

"No." She sobbed, reaching toward him with both hands. "I will be the vines that hold you as you sleep. The greenery at your feet that welcomes you home. The flower that blooms when you smile."

Transformed into something more.

"I will be able to touch you," she said, reaching toward him—forever reaching toward him. "To wrap my arms around your neck." The vines were weaving around her faster now. "A mantle for you to wear to war. Protecting your spine, your flank."

"You will not see me. You will speak no more." He was wrestling with the words, his hands upon his cheeks, lengthening fingernails digging into his flesh.

"But I will always be with you."

To be with him and feel his hand in hers—real flesh instead of an echo... What she wouldn't do for such dreams to come true. But dreams were for the dark of night, of a day long past. Right now she needed him to remain alive.

"I will be with you no matter what form you take," she promised, absolute.

His gaze jerked, and there was something shocked in his expression—some illuminated thought—and he dropped to his knees, ripped open the pouch, shoved some into his mouth, crushed petals in his palms, and finally sunk full hands into the magic diving into the earth. He began to scream.

"No!" she shouted, certain that she was watching him die. The swarming vines suddenly rose, swaying in the sweeping typhoon, and the water of the pond swirled upright behind them like a rippling mirror, impeding every image and view but that of herself.

Your wish, your wish. The power is ours.

"Save Set!"

Your wish, your wish, Sister. We will have it now.

And she knew what they were asking, even here at the end, mimicking what Set had asked her, but even more singular. What do you want? Not a wish that included someone else, but one that solely concerned her.

She opened her mouth, her lips worked, but nothing emerged as she stared at herself in the ripples of the water. What did she see? What did she want? Even though she'd already shared confessions with Set that she'd not allowed herself to think before, it was hard to break free of the deeper, chaining thoughts that had held her for so long.

She didn't fear death—there was no fear of being struck down by the storm winds in the skies, or the magic swirling around her now. But she was held by a type of fear all the same—that thinking anything else, anything new, even within the safety of her mind, would kill all that she was and had once believed in.

The agony of the choice—between past, present, and future—held her immobile, but she looked at her reflection in the whirling water of the pond, and for a moment, she let it all go.

"I wish to choose my own path," she whispered brokenly.

The world shook, again. The old vines chattered in the wind and rubbed with purpose along the moss at the base of the perisim trees. Tales of the dome and a mage capable of wielding the magic of the Nexus would be stories for the next tender. And she would do what she could to aid the unchangeling girl.

The interior vines circled, twining around her shoulders. The tips of the three oldest suddenly arced and thrust down into the soil. The rush of magic was immediate. The vines were calling the magic, pulling the frenzied, uncontrolled rip of it fully toward the Nexus. A dome of a different kind rose again around her.

Set, in full berserker rage, rammed against the barrier, trying to crack it, and all she could feel was relief. He was alive, even as bolts of lightning lit his skin.

She held a hand out to him, instinctively, but a vine wrapped around her wrist and pulled it back to her side. Incomprehension and loss vied with acceptance and regret. This was what she had been preparing for, but it was not quite right. And the magic rushing toward them was not what was supposed to be converted. It could overload the Nexus and kill everything—even the vines.

Set continued to beat against the magic in his fully transformed and completely enraged form; the beast in full power of his body. His gaze met hers, and his eyes were bright with vicious intent. Except, the intent was...focused.

His gaze narrowed in on her. Recognition and identification mixed with emotions she couldn't bear to parse in his eyes.

A bright smile bloomed across her face. Pinpointed control of his berserker form? Able to discern friend from foe? He would be ascendant.

Too late for her to witness it with human eyes, but she would always be with him. She tried to project the thought, the desire, to him with her gaze.

The water of the pond fell over her, cloaked her, then burst into smoke.

A vine pierced her skin, then another. She let out a ragged cry as the razor edges of the leaves cut into her flesh, cutting deeper than ever before. Perhaps this was it. This was how it ended, not by Set or some outside event. It wouldn't be the first time the leykeepers had lied to stabilize the magic taken so long ago.

The plants twined together in sets of green and purple, then pushed inside. She screamed as they dove into her skin, pair after pair in an unending torrent of pain.

And then, suddenly, the pain was gone. The magical storm ceased. The rip between layers closed. And she was lying on the ground staring up at the sky—not a single curved image, false illusion, or dome anywhere in sight.

The garden lay in ruins. The Nexus was silent, but life pulsed within and around her. Whispers shivered along her skin.

And she...she understood.

The Nexus was now dormant, but there was one final conduit left.

Running her fingers along the nearly invisible hair on her arms, she could hear the whispers of the vines and feel their raised veins beneath her flesh.

Did we do well? Are you pleased?

She pushed herself into a sitting position and looked down. The vines were tattooed stripes on her skin, pulsing green with the beat of her heart. Transforming her into an eternal conduit, one not trapped inside a particular space. They had called to the exploding magic, called it here and used it to destroy the garden and transform her.

The leykeepers had weakened the seals, and a faraway mage had loosed the magic, but it was Lirah's companions who had harnessed the opportunity and turned it into a gift, and it was she who had chosen.

Are you pleased, Sister?

"Yes," she said, brokenly and with feeling.

The air where the dome had been was clear—leaving but a faint echo of the barrier that had once trapped the magic inside.

"Lirah. Come." Set, in his massive berserker form and dripping in blood, held out a clawed hand—the claws of his most vicious form—urging her away from the Nexus.

"You are free, too," she said, her breath catching. "You are in control."

"Yes. Lirah, you must step across now."

She looked at the wide golden arcs in the ground where the dome had once connected, wondering why he hadn't crossed the barrier and simply carried her off.

"Tender," said a harsh voice. She jerked her gaze in the direction. Five of the leykeepers were still unconscious, but three of them were brokenly pulling themselves to their feet.

"Lirah." Set beckoned more quickly.

"Do not do it, Tender," the Southwestern Leykeeper warned.

"Do not, Tender, please," the Northwestern Leykeeper begged.

She looked back at Set, at the place where he still stood, across the barrier that had once stood between them.

"You must do it," Set said, voice urgent but turning bleak, as if he feared her answer. "I cannot choose this for you."

Slowly she reached out her hand to test the barrier that had always existed above the circle.

"Tender, do not! You will end us all!"

She retracted her fingers, curling them into her palms, and looked behind her at the Nexus, now motionless and dormant in the center of a silent field.

Then she looked down at her own skin, swirling with the green and gold of the garden's magic. The vines swam under her skin in exuberant excitement. Together! Together! The garden will go where you choose. To stay or go.

She looked back at Set. He didn't say anything more, even as his eyes—becoming more human as the magic of the event started to recede around them—held something close to desperation now as the conscious leykeepers stumbled across the ground to reset their amulets.

Set's hand remained extended, a clear offering, and a choice.

Her fingers extended hesitantly across the space and her breath hitched as her palm touched his. Fingers—rough with battle earned calluses and half-healing scars, but warm with welcome—wrapped protectively around hers.

His dark gaze was full of promise and deep emotion, and his hand was wrapped in hers.

She took a step toward him, and stepped through the barrier into the world beyond.

And together, they changed their world.

About the Author

Anne Zoelle loves writing about college-aged protagonists who get embroiled in complicated adventures. Split between the midwest and west coast, she writes books for all ages that feature sentient libraries, rock guardians, and people finding family.

You can find her at www.annezoelle.com.